BRAZOS STATION

Caleb Brett liked his job as deputy sheriff and being betrothed to the sheriff's daughter, Rose. What he didn't like was the thought of the sheriff moving in with them once they were married. But capturing the infamous outlaw Gil Bannerman offered a way out because there was plenty of reward money. Then came Brett's big mistake — he lost Bannerman and was framed. Now everything he treasured was lost. Did he have a chance in hell of fighting his way back?

Books by Clayton Nash
in the Linford Western Library:

DAKOTA WOLF
LONG-RIDING MAN
THE MUSTANG STRIP

CLAYTON NASH

BRAZOS STATION

Complete and Unabridged

LINFORD
Leicester

First published in Great Britain in 1998 by
Robert Hale Limited
London

First Linford Edition
published 1999
by arrangement with
Robert Hale Limited
London

British Library CIP Data

Nash, Clayton
Brazos Station.—Large print ed.—
Linford western library
1. Western stories
2. Large type books
I. Title
823.9′14 [F]

ISBN 0–7089–5434–0

Published by
F. A. Thorpe (Publishing) Ltd.
Anstey, Leicestershire

Set by Words & Graphics Ltd.
Anstey, Leicestershire
Printed and bound in Great Britain by
T. J. International Ltd., Padstow, Cornwall

This book is printed on acid-free paper

1

Capture of a Badman

Deputy Caleb Brett wrenched at the reins of his galloping bay gelding, ducking at the same time as the low branch of the tree swept down his back. It knocked his hat off but it hung by the tie-thong as he weaved the racing animal through the brush, glimpsing his quarry no more than sixty yards up-slope.

The man above snapped his head around as he put his long-stepping black across an open section of the ridge, sliding it slightly down-grade into the closest bush. His face seemed white but there was no actual fear there. Just before the black smashed into the brush line, Gil Bannerman whipped his Colt from his cross-draw holster and thumbed two racketing shots at the pursuing lawman.

Brett lay flat along the bay's straining neck, heard one bullet rattle through the branches above him, the second whine away in ricochet to his left. By then Bannerman was plunging into the brush but Brett straightened, sliding his Winchester carbine from the saddle boot. He flung it to his shoulder, reins between his teeth, as he triggered three fast shots into the brush just as Bannerman disappeared from sight.

Cursing, Brett sheathed the smoking gun and slammed the bay towards the brush. But there was turmoil of some kind over there and he slowed, frowning puzzledly. Then he saw what had happened and he smiled thinly through the caked dust masking his lower face.

His shots had missed Bannerman, but apparently one at least had found the black and the big animal was going down. It rolled sideways on the downgrade and the deputy glimpsed Bannerman's body flailing wildly as the man was hurled from the saddle. He hit a good ten feet downslope with the black tumbling and sliding towards him. Bannerman managed to somersault, hurting one wrist in the process, flung himself desperately aside as the floundering, whinnying horse slid past, legs kicking. One hoof caught him on the left shoulder, sent him spinning. He used the momentum to hurl himself away from the wounded animal, then let his legs fold as his boots struck the slope. He snapped them straight instantly and his body shot above the brush for brief seconds before he dived into the thicket out of sight.

By that time, Brett was crashing the protesting bay through the brush, the horse's hoofs sliding, forelegs straight, haunches going down towards the ground in a long slide. Brett had the carbine in his right hand, standing in the stirrups with the ease of an expert horseman, left hand manipulating the reins. He saw a flash of sun-faded red — Bannerman's shirt. It was off to his left and much farther down than he would have believed possible. Hell, Bannerman must be *flying*!

He triggered a shot one-handed, having no real hope of his lead finding target, but it would keep Bannerman running and if he kept up his present pace he was sure to fall and tumble. But Bannerman somehow held his pace and stayed on his feet, arms smashing at the branches that whipped across his face, tore his clothes. Still it was only a matter of time and when Brett saw him fall he smiled thinly, heaving his thundering mount towards the fugitive.

Bannerman bounced to his feet again and hurled himself downslope once more, but he had slowed and, what was more important, Brett had gained five yards and was only that distance behind him now. Bannerman glanced back once, face strained and scratched and sweat flying from his blond hair. He didn't reach for his gun as Brett half expected, but propped suddenly as the deputy spurred the bay in for the kill and by then the animal was committed and hurtled past him in a headlong plunge towards the river below. Brett cursed and spun the carbine around the trigger guard, jacking another shell into the breech. He fired beneath his left arm. It was a lucky shot although it missed Bannerman. But the slug exploded a handful of bark from the trunk of a sapling right in front of the man and Bannerman clawed at his face as the splinters and sap stung him.

He floundered, staggered, hit another sapling and cannoned off at an angle. He fell and rolled and when he straightened again, he found himself in the shallows of the river.

Brett had hauled rein and was spurring the panting bay towards him, sunlight catching the fans of spray as the horse made one final effort. Bannerman staggered as he heaved upright, snatching at his six-gun.

The holster was empty.

He must have lost the weapon during

the headlong flight down the slope. Gasping, only half-seeing, he spun and staggered out into the river, figuring to try for the other side where he saw some dead limbs of trees lying on the bank. He might be able to use one as a weapon . . .

Thunder and splashing filled his head as he pounded through water that was up to his knees now. Curses swirled in his brain as he realized the mistake he had made: the deeper water was slowing him down.

Then the bay reached him and he was trampled down under water, coughing and choking as he rose. Brett came flying out of the saddle, his hard, muscular body smashing into the outlaw and driving him back under water. Panic seized Bannerman as he swallowed water and sand, choking. He thrashed frantically, flailing with clawed hands. One caught the deputy in the left eye and Brett wrenched his head, losing his momentum and spilling sideways.

Bannerman either saw his predicament

or sensed it, flung himself at the lawman, reaching for the carbine. Brett hurled it from him, heard it splash into the shallows, lifted his legs into Bannerman's chest. The man grunted and Brett flung him from him, fighting to get to his feet, the river dragging him down. The bay was still plunging about and he stumbled into it, was thrown backwards to fall on his back. Bannerman lunged at him, a river rock in his right hand, lifting above his head, face contorted with the frenzy of killing. Brett wrenched his head aside, felt the concussion of the rock smashing into the water beside his ear. Head ringing, he looped a right across, felt his knuckles grinding into Bannerman's neck. The man fell but threw the rock. It bounced off Brett's shoulder, numbing his arm briefly, and then the deputy was on his feet and as Bannerman hastily scrambled to hands and knees, Brett swung his boot up under the man's jaw.

Bannerman was hurled back six feet,

arms wide and flailing futilely. He landed on his back and his head lolled as he sank.

Gasping, barely able to stay on his feet, Brett fumbled at the man's torn red shirt, found a grip, and heaved him towards the bank where the bay was shaking the river out of its coat. He made a long, strangled sound as he flung the unconscious Bannerman onto the bank and collapsed beside the man, chest heaving, head spinning, red and white lights whirling behind his eyes.

But moments later he crawled to where the bay stood, hauled himself to his feet by one foreleg and fumbled in his saddlebags.

He knelt beside the stirring Bannerman again and clamped the manacles on the man's wrists behind his back.

Bannerman grunted, the pain of the metal biting into his flesh making his eyes snap open. They seemed glazed and out of focus for a few moments and then they settled on Deputy Caleb Brett's face as the man wiped it free of mud and sand with a sodden kerchief.

'Wh . . . where you from?' the outlaw gasped.

'Las Cruces,' Brett said, his words slurred.

Bannerman frowned. 'Don't tell . . . me . . . you just . . . happened on . . . me in Wagonmound?'

Brett smiled slowly despite his fatigue and hurts. 'Galls like hell, don't it? Yeah — just seen you coming outta the livery. Light caught you right. You looked just like you do on the Wanted dodger pinned to the wall behind my desk.'

Bannerman cursed. 'Knew I shouldn'ta stayed so long with that damn whore! But she was French, man, and I'd never had lovin' like that before. Well, my pappy warned me about thinking below my belt instead of with my head . . . But don't think it's gonna be easy getting me back to Las Cruces, deputy . . . You gotta name?'

'Caleb Brett.'

Bannerman nodded slowly, rubbing

his throbbing, swelling jaw gently, awkwardly on one shoulder. 'Heard of you . . . Hunted down Cass Larue, didn't you?' Brett didn't say anything. 'Yeah, you're the one. Went into his camp, gunned down three of his pards an' took old Cass back to stand trial and hang. Well, be advised as of this moment, Deputy Caleb Brett, that *I* don't aim to hang. Fact, don't aim to die at all yet a spell . . . So you and me're gonna butt heads long before you sight Las Cruces, savvy?'

Brett shook his head slowly. 'No — reckon not, Bannerman. The only head-butting you and me're gonna do is this!'

And on the last word, Brett's right hand swung up and across and the side of his heavy Colt Peacemaker smashed across Bannerman's temple with the force of a mule kick.

The outlaw's feet left the ground completely before he fell in a tumbled heap on the river bank, one leg trailing in the muddy water.

Bannerman was as good as his word: he made things as hard as possible for Brett to take him back to Las Cruces.

They stayed overnight just south of the state line at the old abandoned staging outpost called Brazos Station. It was well north of the river of that name but it had been where southbound travellers changed stages to either keep going in that direction to El Paso and all points east and west, or at Brazos Station they could choose their own direction and eventually be able to link up with the new railroad that went to Tucson, Arizona, after starting at San Antonio, Texas.

The place hadn't been deserted for more than a few months and yet already sand had piled high against the adobe walls of the old waystation. A large door had sprung and now sagged on a single hinge in the stables building.

The stone wall surrounding the well

was crumbled a little in one part but the winch and rope were still operable. Brett looked down into the deep hole and decided the water could be poisoned. He was glad he had topped up the canteens at the river where he had captured Gil Bannerman. No use taking chances . . .

On the way in they rode double because Brett had had to put Bannerman's wounded black out of its misery after the fight at the river. This had given the killer the chance to snap his head back when they were approaching a dry wash, his skull catching Brett in the mouth — he had meant it to smash the deputy's nose but he was slightly off, otherwise he might have pulled off his attempt to escape.

As it was, Brett reeled, tasting blood as his lips mashed against his teeth. He clutched wildly at the reins and Bannerman hipped as far as he could, ramming his upper body into Brett. The added weight flung the lawman from the saddle and Bannerman laughed, settled back and kicked the bay with his heels as the deputy rolled in the dust.

The horse didn't move and Bannerman swore savagely.

'C'mon, you piece of crowbait! *Move*! You son of a bitch!'

Sitting up, a mite dazed, Brett grimaced, put two fingers in his bloody mouth and whistled piercingly. The bay reared, whinnying, and Bannerman yelled as he was flung off to land heavily in the dust only a yard or two from the lawman. Brett clambered casually to his feet, dusted himself down with his hat and stood over the outlaw, fumbling out a kerchief.

He dabbed at his mouth, speaking around the wadded cloth. 'That was two tries in one, Bannerman — Your first and your last.'

'Don't bet on it!' Bannerman struggled to his feet, manacled hands behind his back making it difficult.

'You got any sense, you'll mind what I say.' Brett called the bay to him, patted his neck, managed to find a cube of sugar in a vest pocket and the horse snapped it up. 'Me and Zack have an understanding. No one rides him but me.'

Bannerman's eyes were red and murderous as he looked at the bay. 'That's another thing I wouldn't bet on, Brett!'

The deputy kicked Bannerman's legs from under him and he fell with a grunt to the ground again. Brett tapped the man with his gun barrel and while he was dazed, took off the manacles and locked them on Bannerman's wrists in front of him. The outlaw blinked and held up his hands, puzzled. Brett took his lariat, made a couple of turns around the linking chain of the cuffs and knotted it off. He mounted the bay and looped the rope around the saddlehorn, hanging the spare coils. He nudged the bay forward and the slack was soon taken up and Bannerman was jerked forward. He yelled, swearing as he struggled to get his legs under him, stumbling and staggering behind the animal.

When he was upright, more or less, Brett increased his pace so that Bannerman was jogging down into the dry wash, falling twice, dragged through loose dust and over some hard-baked clay before managing to get to his feet again . . .

So it was just before sundown when they reached Brazos Station. By then, Bannerman was barely able to stand, gasping heavily. Brett put the bay in the stables, leaving the outlaw roped to the hitchrail in front of the main building. He rubbed down the bay and fed it oats and some grass he pulled up and watered it before returning to Bannerman.

'Do I get to eat, too?' the outlaw growled as Brett walked on by, shouldering his saddle.

'Could be.'

Brett went into the main building, got a fire going in the old rusted range and cooked up sowbelly and beans and three eggs he'd found in the stables where a couple of abandoned chickens had obviously made their home. The coffee was fresh and strong and bitter: he had bought a new bag of beans in Wagonmound before commencing his chase of Gil Bannerman.

He roped the outlaw to an upright in the main room, wrapping the rope around and around the man's torso, leaving his hands and arms free, but shackling his ankles. Bannerman ate hungrily. Brett took his time at the old battered table where stage passengers had taken their meals not so long ago. There was oil in two of the four swinging lamps and he lit one of these.

'I got you scared, huh?' Bannerman asked as Brett rolled a cigarette and licked the paper. He fired up, got up and placed it between the outlaw's lips, standing over the man while he rolled and lit a smoke for himself.

'You've never scared me, Bannerman — I might be scared I'll lose you, that's all.'

Bannerman smiled crookedly. 'Keep it that way, deputy. You'll never bring me to trial. I got friends who'll see to that.'

'You mean the ones you haven't already killed?' Bannerman made a habit of abandoning his friends or killing them if it would help his own escape from a tight corner.

The blond outlaw shrugged. 'I know too much about too many people for 'em to let me go on trial.'

Brett sat down on one of the hard forms, forearms resting on his knees. 'Maybe that means they'll try to stop you getting to court — with a bullet.'

Bannerman seemed briefly surprised at the suggestion, then shook his head, smiling crookedly. 'Nah — I got it all written down. Kept in a safe place with a lawyer friend of mine. Somethin' happens to me and the package is opened and . . . ' He shrugged expressively.

Brett smoked silently.

'You'll be in the Las Cruces lock-up

before any of your pards know you've been captured.'

'That's what you figure, huh?' When Brett made no reply, Bannerman said, a little tightly, 'Where you think I was headed outta Wagonmound? Just seein' the country? Uh-uh, Brett — I had me a rendezvous. I don't arrive and someone'll come lookin'.'

'And all they'll find is a corpse,' Brett said standing abruptly, stabbing out his cigarette butt on the table edge. He moved fast and before Bannerman realized what was happening, his hands were in manacles again. 'They attempt to break you free, Bannerman, and you get the first bullet — So you better pray your friends *don't* come after you. Sleep well.'

'Hey! I can't sleep like this!'

Brett drew his pistol and hefted it. 'Like a sedative?'

Bannerman scowled and saw a faint smile on Brett's face just before the man blew out the lamp.

During the night he worked on the

ropes around his torso and just before the first streak of grey lightened the east the coils fell around him loosely. He struggled to get out of them and after he'd sweated and muttered a while he managed it, eased away from the post and started to stand.

'If you're aiming to take a leak, I'll come with you,' Brett said casually from his soogan which he had spread in a corner. He smiled at the startled outlaw in the faint light. 'I been listening to you working on them ropes half the night. You're stupid, Bannerman. You needed your sleep because you're walking again today.'

Bannerman sobbed a string of curses, spun around, swinging up his manacled hands as he rushed the deputy. Brett tripped him and Bannerman slammed into the wall, slipping down to his knees, gasping, dazed.

Brett hauled him upright by his belt and pushed him stumblingly towards the door.

'Las Cruces next stop, Bannerman.'

The blond outlaw turned to the lawman, his face contorted with hate.

'You ain't gonna live that long, you son of a bitch!'

★ ★ ★

But, although Bannerman tried twice more to escape and made one attempt to kill Brett with a piece of deadwood, the deputy dragged the exhausted, ragged outlaw into the main street of Las Cruces and dumped him in the cells.

When he went back to the front office, Sheriff Morg Blackman was waiting, hatless, carrying his gunbelt in his hand, having seen Brett ride in from his front window. His shirt tails weren't even tucked in properly.

'Did I see right or was that Gil Bannerman under all that dust at the end of your rope?'

'He's in Cell Two,' Brett said, hanging his hat on a peg and sitting down at his cluttered desk in one corner. He yawned and locked his fingers, lifting his arms above his head as he stretched some of the kinks out of his muscles. 'I'll get my report done and then I aim to sleep for a couple of days.'

'Judas, Caleb, the marshals've been after this sonuver for months! Ever since he killed that army payroll escort . . . There could be a big reward!'

Brett looked soberly at the older lawman, knowing how the man was thinking. As sheriff, he would be entitled to fifty per cent of any reward and the sheriff's retirement was only a couple of years away. He longed for a small spread of his own and half of a big bounty would help him get it.

Brett's face showed nothing but he couldn't help thinking that that would be fine with him. Because he was aiming to marry Rose, Blackman's daughter, and if the sheriff didn't have a place of his own to retire to, it would mean he would come and live with them. He felt kind of ashamed to be thinking such things but having worked every day of four years with Blackman, spending the rest of his life with the man under the same roof held little appeal. It had been the cause of several arguments between himself and Rose already . . .

'We'll see, Morg,' Brett said, dipping a pen into the stone bottle and beginning to head up his report.

Blackman buckled on his gunbelt after tucking in his shirt tails, ran a tongue around his lips, and said, 'I better go an' notify the marshal's office in San Antone seein' as you nabbed him on Texas soil . . . You git your rest, boy, after you finish that report. I'll look after the rest of it . . . '

Brett watched the sheriff hurry out into the early, dust-hazed light of Main. Sure, he'd get off a wire to San Antone — but his first stop would be the saloon. Brett shook his head, trying to push thoughts of what lay ahead in his own life from his mind as he filled out his report.

If he'd thought about the reward side of things, maybe he wouldn't have even bothered to run down Bannerman at all . . . Morg Blackman could well end up as his neighbour, damnit!

He tightened his lips and wrote faster.

It seemed that every move he made lately was wrong.

2

Brazos Station

'You'll be famous, Caleb,' Rose Blackman said, clinging to Brett's left arm — it had taken her a long time to remember never to hang onto his gun-arm. 'Dad's already talking about retiring early so you can be sheriff and he can start building on that section just across the ridge from our place.'

Brett groaned inwardly. He had figured something like this when Blackman had spent a small fortune on telegraph messages to find out that Wells Fargo, suppliers of the stolen army payroll and therefore its insurers, were offering seven-and-a-half thousand dollars reward for the capture and conviction of Gil Bannerman.

The sheriff had also learned that Bannerman had bounties on his head in three other states. He was presently filing claims for them in his own and Brett's names and was making wild calculations, deciding they would both receive something like eight thousand dollars.

Brett shuddered at the thought. Such a sum would enable Morg Blackman to buy the section next to the one he was paying off so that after the wedding he and Rose would have a home waiting for them. When he had found some spare time he had started building a log cabin and was making good progress, although he still owed plenty for the lumber and stock.

But suddenly the project lost some of its appeal. The thought of Morg Blackman only just across the ridge knocked the edge off his enthusiasm. Morg was a man in his fifties, had been battling the bottle most of his life, and it was only because he had neither enough money nor time that he wasn't a full-time drunk. He was also a whiner.

But if he collected half the reward monies and had nothing much to do with his time except work on his spread — Well, Brett knew the old sheriff well enough to realize there never would be a spread that would pay its way and let him live tolerably comfortable years in the winter of his life. Morg would find excuses not to do this chore or that, and find just as many other excuses to ride into town and have a drink or two with his cronies in the bar of the *La Bella* saloon . . .

Rose would start worrying about him, insist that he take his meals with them, likely, finally have him move in . . .

He despised himself for thinking such thoughts about the man who had given him a deputy's star when he had been on the drift and broke, but he had figured out long ago that Morg Blackman had made him deputy so as to make his own job easier, not for any other reason.

Brett had bought into a fight that

could have ended in Morg's death and the sheriff had been quick enough to see that Brett was handy with fists and gun and had a high proportion of steel in his backbone. Blackman had already been going down-hill at that time and was in danger of losing his job because of the lawlessness of the town.

After hiring Brett, the law had been enforced properly and now Las Cruces was the most law-abiding town in south-west New Mexico. Law-abiding and *safe*.

Now Rose jarred his arm and said, 'Brett! I'm talking to you!'

'Sorry, hon — Pretty blamed tired after that ride up from Texas. Couldn't risk much sleep with someone like Bannerman in tow.'

'Oh, I'm sorry, dear! It was thoughtless of me keeping you out like this. You go on back to your room and go to bed ... There'll be plenty of time for us to talk and plan.'

'Plan? I thought we'd made all our plans . . . ?'

'I mean if Dad does manage to buy that section next to us . . . We'll have to . . . modify some of our ideas, I think.'

His frown deepened and he could see her lovely face in the dim light coming from the door of the sheriff's rented cottage, but it was a little strained now and he figured she was just as relieved as he was not to have to continue with the present conversation. Not right now, leastways . . .

She planted a kiss on his deeply tanned cheek. 'Off you go and rest, Caleb — I'll see you tomorrow.'

'Yeah — 'Night, hon,' he said a mite absently and walked back towards the jailhouse. He used the small room behind the law office, and he shuffled his feet some through the dust as he made his way there, head down.

Hell, as if he didn't have enough troubles with a man like Bannerman in his charge, without this spectre of

Morg Blackman's retirement raising its head to torment him.

'Ah, hell,' he said aloud as he unlocked the jailhouse door. 'I'll be old myself one day, and if I have a daughter I guess I'll be looking to her to take care of me.'

But he knew he wouldn't: it wasn't his way. He was too independent and proud, always had been . . .

He checked on Bannerman, double-checked the bars and locks on the jailhouse doors, and then locked up the front office and turned in.

He had a restless night, haunted by visions of a drunken Morg Blackman sleeping in the big feather bed between himself and Rose.

* * *

'Why the hell do they want to meet me at Brazos Station?' Brett frowned down at the wire that Morg Blackman had just handed him. 'The first arrangement to make the transfer here with two

29

marshals coming to collect him was much safer.'

Blackman, red-eyed and his breath already smelling of whiskey at nine in the morning, scratched his scalp beneath his stringy, lank, colourless hair and shrugged. 'I dunno — Mebbe they figure he has to be delivered onto Texas soil, seein' as that's where he was first took. You should've turned him over to the marshals while you were down there, Caleb.'

Brett looked exasperated. 'It'd have taken me a week to get to San Antone, four days to El Paso. I didn't fancy spending that much time on those trails with Bannerman. That's his old stamping ground around that part of Texas.'

'Yeah, well, that's what the marshals want so we have to do what they say — I don't want nothin' to go wrong that might hold up the reward comin' through.'

Brett was still frowning at the yellow telegraph form. 'Well, like you say we have to follow their orders, but it ain't anything I'm looking forward to . . . You get the names of the marshals who're s'posed to collect Bannerman?'

Blackman had to look them up, searched through scattered papers on his desk, muttering something about an old man's memory before he finally found what he was looking for.

'Marshals Foran and McMurphy — I know Lin McMurphy. Good lawman.'

'Gimme his description, Morg.' At the sheriff's puzzled look, Brett added, 'I just want to make sure I'm handing over Bannerman to the right man.'

'Hell's sake, of course you will be — Well, I ain't seen McMurphy in ten, twelve years, right at the end of the war, matter of fact. But he's big and rawboned, has — had — sandy hair, a kinda lantern jaw. Think his eyes were grey — or was it blue? Could've been kinda blue-green if I recollect correctly . . . '

Brett sighed. 'Leave it at that, Morg.

He could be bald and fat as a beer keg by now . . . You gonna help me escort Bannerman down to Brazos Station?'

Morg's fading eyebrows shot upwards towards his receding hair line. 'Me? Hell, I can't leave the town without a lawman, Caleb, you know that! I s'pose I could call up a posse of volunteers to go along with you — But they might be able to claim some of the reward, you know.'

'Yeah, well we wouldn't want to share it around too much, would we?' Brett said, his bitter tone lost on the sheriff. 'I'll do it. I brought him in alone, I'll take him down to meet the marshals alone.'

'When you leavin'?' Blackman asked eagerly.

'You make out the transfer papers, Morg, and I'll go get a mount for Bannerman and load a packmule.'

'OK — You could be away by noon.'

Brett hesitated, then nodded. Why not? He'd be glad to get away from

Las Cruces for a spell.

He had a lot of thinking to do, not much of it to his liking.

* * *

There were folk in Las Cruces who would have liked to lynch Bannerman because of his crimes and it didn't surprise Caleb Brett any that the man was stoned as he led him out of town.

He had tried to keep to back streets but the word had spread that Bannerman was here and the men had been watching. Bannerman jerked his head as stones thudded against his upper arms and chest, yelling profanity at the shouting men. When a rock knocked off his hat and blood crawled down his face from a gash in his scalp, Brett drew his Peacemaker and put a couple of shots over the heads of the tormentors, scattering them.

'Too bad you didn't do that ten minutes ago!' snapped Bannerman, blood dripping from his jaw.

'They deserve the chance to let off a little steam.'

'You better hope I don't bust loose, deputy! I'll tear your goddamn head off if I do!'

Brett set the man's hat on his head again after seeing that the gash wasn't serious. Most of the other wounds would only leave a bruise or two. 'First sign of you even trying to bust loose and I'll put a bullet through you, Bannerman. I won't kill you, but you'd be a fool to try to escape with a shattered kneecap.'

Bannerman remained silent but his face was full of burning hatred.

They cleared Las Cruces and Brett kept checking their backtrail until they reached the foothills. Once there, he went deep into the timber and dropped down into narrow arroyos, angling south-west until he reached a treed slope and lifted up to the high pass. Once through there — after a cold night spent amongst the rocks without a fire or warm food — they dropped down again, left the San Andres behind and entered the wilderness of the Sacramento Range.

'Takin' the long way round, ain't you?' complained Bannerman, who seemed to have given up trying to shuck his shackles and manacles.

'We could take the usual trail — and make you a target if you like,' Brett told him and the outlaw fell into sullen silence again.

Brett felt uneasy, several times halting and staking out Bannerman's mount and the pack-mule while he scouted ahead. The trail seemed clear, but he couldn't shake the feeling that there was danger, a lot of danger, surrounding him.

But he saw no one, although there was a smudge of grey on a far ridge that was likely smoke. There was little of it so maybe it was only an Indian campfire or that of a mountain man: there were still a few who hunted cougars and the odd bear in the Sacramentos.

He didn't get much sleep the second

night out, stashed his prisoner amongst rocks above a fake campsite with bedrolls under blankets in the shadows just beyond the dying fire. He sat with his carbine across his thighs, dozing most of the night, feeling like he hadn't rested at all by the time daylight came.

Bannerman smiled crookedly at him as they ate a cold breakfast. 'Kinda rattled, ain't you, deputy?'

'You're still my first target if any of your pards show, Bannerman,' Brett told the man coldly and Bannerman lost the smile pronto.

They came within sight of Brazos Station before noon and Brett halted, climbed a high rock and scanned the abandoned stage depot with a pair of field glasses. He said nothing when he came down, stowed the glasses in his saddlebags and mounted the bay.

'Well?' snapped Bannerman impatiently.

'They're there . . . Four horses in the corrals, two saddles draped over the top rail, pack frames on the porch.

I kind of expected the marshals to send more than two men for you, Bannerman.'

'Mebbe they'll wish they had.'

Brett said nothing, picked up the lead ropes and started out of the rocks but suddenly stopped, hipping in the saddle and looking at the frowning Bannerman thoughtfully.

The outlaw tensed, looked mighty uncomfortable.

'What?' he demanded. 'What're you plannin' now, damn you?'

* * *

The two men came sauntering out onto the sandswept porch of the old stage station, cradling guns in their arms. The tall lean one held a rifle, the other, wide-shouldered, bearded, carried a Greener shotgun, his stubby thumb resting on the hammer. He squinted at the foothills.

'I see mebbe three hosses, but is that only one rider?'

The lean man nodded slowly. 'That'll be Brett.'

'Where the hell's Bannerman?' The hammers on the shotgun notched back to full cock.

'Easy. He's tricky and he's hard. Let's see what he has to say.' They waited until Brett was starting in past the old lodgepole gate and the lean man called out. 'You deputy Brett?'

'One and the same — Who'm I talking to?'

'Well, wouldn't 'xactly call it talkin' right now, but I'm Marv Foran and this here's McMurphy.'

Brett stopped his bay several yards out from the main building, holding the reins casually in his left hand with the lead ropes of the other animals — Bannerman's horse and the pack-mule — but his right hand stayed on his thigh, not far from his six-gun.

'You gents mind telling me your badge numbers? You first, McMurphy.'

The broad-shouldered man scowled past Foran, who nodded impatiently.

McMurphy started to pull his badge out from his shirt to check the number but Brett said, 'Uh-uh. Man who's been in the Marshals long as you ought to know it by heart, McMurphy.'

The marshal glared, covering his badge with one big hand, casually swinging up the cocked shotgun barrels. 'How's one, three, seven, dash D sound?'

'Sounds like the one I was given.' Brett had wired for the marshal's number himself after receiving the first telegraph message. 'How about you, Foran?'

'Nine-four, dash B.' Foran spoke quickly, confidently, boring his gaze into Brett. 'Now let's see some identification from you.'

Brett nodded and dropped the reins, using his left hand to reach up and push his vest aside to show his deputy's badge.

'If that ain't got your name on it, it don't count for much,' Foran said.

'Guess you're right — Well, I've got

the papers on Bannerman and a pay-slip from Las Cruces County . . . '

'Hell, never mind all this palaver,' snapped McMurphy. 'Where the hell's Bannerman?'

Brett jerked his head over his shoulder. 'Back there. I stashed him. Wiped out my tracks. You could search till sundown and not find him.'

'The hell're you tryin' to pull, Brett?' asked Foran, growing impatient, too. 'We ain't makin' no search for him!'

Brett looked from one to the other. 'Like you gents to explain why the hand-over was changed to this place instead of you men coming to Las Cruces. This is kind of outta the way and while I see only your two mounts and pack-horses in the corrals, there are a lot more hoofprints around the corral and leading out of the yard . . . Whenever you're ready, gents.'

He smiled without humour as he waited, right hand still on his thigh close to his holstered Peacemaker.

Foran shook his head slowly, and

sighed. 'Well, they told us you was leery — Look, we do what we're told. Chief Marshal said pick up Bannerman at Brazos Station, then go meet the train at Briscoe Sidin' and ride it back to San Antone. And that's what we aim to do. It's the safest way.'

Brett thought about it, gave no indication whether he accepted the explanation or not, then asked, 'And the extra hoofprints?'

'Judas priest!' gritted McMurphy, stirring restlessly, but Foran answered readily enough.

'We made 'em. Rode in early, then figured we oughta take a looksee around, so rode out again, hit the foothills and watched the trails. We seen you way back on that trail down from the high pass, then rode back here to wait . . . ' Then his voice hardened. 'Only you ain't brought us Bannerman. Time for games is over, Brett. Let's get to it.'

Covered by the marshals' guns, Brett sat back in the saddle, lips pursed, then nodded. 'Be right back.'

'Wait up!' Foran snapped. 'You don't go nowhere without us!'

'One of you can take Bannerman's horse. I ain't waiting while you saddle up those mounts in the corrals.'

Foran jerked his head at McMurphy and the big man reluctantly lowered the hammers on the shot-gun and stepped down to swing aboard the horse used earlier by Bannerman. Riding out of the yard beside Brett, the shotgun barrels pointing in the deputy's direction, McMurphy said, 'You could get to be a pain, Brett.'

'So I've been told — You must've been pretty young when you joined the Marshals, McMurphy.' At the man's wary glance he added, 'Well, Morg Blackman said he knew you during the war. You can't be that old.'

McMurphy allowed himself a crooked smile. 'That was my old man. He was killed two, no three years back now — Bushwhacked in the back of the head. I'd joined about six years ago and when he died I took his badge number — That satisfy you?'

Brett nodded and then pushed the bay ahead, leading the marshal through narrow crevices until he came to the one, way back at the end of a coulee, where he had trussed up Bannerman, gag and all. The outlaw was fuming when Brett dragged him out and yanked the gag loose, leaving him in manacles and shackles. Bannerman swore loud and long, lunged for McMurphy, trying to grab his six-gun from its holster.

The marshal moved fast for a man of his bulk and slammed the shotgun butt against the side of the outlaw's head, beating Bannerman to his knees. The man swayed there, dazed, fresh blood flowing down one side of his face.

'Better get him across the saddle and ride double,' Brett said as McMurphy glared.

'I know my job.'

Back at the old stage station, while Bannerman lay on the porch amongst the piled sand and grit, the lawmen exchanged papers and signatures. Brett stepped back, nodding.

'He's all yours, gents.' He flicked his gaze to Bannerman, who was watching him bleakly. 'See you in hell, Bannerman.'

'You'll see me before that! When I come for you, you son of a bitch!' Bannerman spat and Foran laughed briefly.

'Only movin' you'll be doin' is dancin' at the end of a rope, so shut your mouth before I turn Mac loose on you to give you some dental work with the butt of his shotgun.'

Bannerman glared. 'I won't forget you, neither! Nor this fat sonuver!'

McMurphy kicked him between the shoulders and Bannerman buried his face in the loose sand, rolling aside to spit and hawk.

Brett shook hands briefly with the tough marshals and mounted his bay. 'Hope you get him back all right — Morg Blackman's waiting on his share of the reward money.'

'Yeah, too bad we don't qualify — We'll let you know soon as they convict him and set a hangin' date. Try and get down to see it if you can. I'll buy you a drink.'

Brett merely nodded, caught the edge of McMurphy's bleak stare and wheeled his bay, leading the pack-mule out of the windswept yard of Brazos Station.

* * *

Caleb Brett had been back in Las Cruces for two days when word came in with a trail herder that Indians were on the loose once more in the south-west.

'Reckon it's a few young bucks busted outta the reservation,' the man told the drinkers in the *La Bella* saloon. 'Ran off some cows and hit that Briscoe Siding. Killed the railroad man and the telegraph operator, then burned it down.'

'How long ago?' asked the barkeep, wanting to keep the man talking

45

because other drinkers had crowded close to hear and were ordering while they listened.

'Reckon it musta been about a week . . . '

When Brett heard he frowned, looked across his desk at Morg Blackman who had drifted into the saloon in time to hear the end of the trail man's story.

'That must've been before Foran and McMurphy got there to pick up the train . . . Wait a minute! Damn, I should've checked before this!' He rummaged in his desk drawer and brought out a tattered brochure put out by the *Texas-Pacific Railroad*. He leafed swiftly through it, and looked up grim-faced.

'There wasn't any train going to San Antone within four days of my handing over Bannerman . . . The marshals wouldn't've camped out with him that long — Goddamnit, Morg, I *knew* there was something odd about those two.'

Blackman was pale-faced, no doubt thinking about the reward money. 'Well, McMurphy had a son, all right, and the badge numbers checked — *and* they had the right papers. What more did you want?'

'I dunno. I had a hunch that something wasn't right . . . Even waited in the foothills until they left with Bannerman. They had him still shackled, all right . . . '

'Will you for hell's sake quit all this worryin', Caleb?' Blackman was growing angry now, resenting his deputy making him feel unsure about the fate of the reward money. 'Everything's OK, I tell you.'

Brett reached down for his hat and jammed it on his head. 'Yeah, well I'm gonna send a wire to the San Antone marshal's office and see if Bannerman arrived safely . . . '

'Look, don't go doin' a thing like that! They won't like you checkin' up that way. Makes 'em look bad!'

Brett shouldered past the sheriff and

hurried down to the telegraph office. Hal Wishart, the operator, was just getting out of his chair, taking off his green eyeshade, holding a message form.

'Hey, was just comin' to see you, Caleb — Look at this, man! That ol' mountain man, Farley, had his bear dog tore up by a grizzly and buried him in the mountains . . . Then come down outta the foothills and made his way to the old Brazos Station, aimin' to camp there before headin' out someplace that sold booze. He sure was partial to that old hound and I guess it hit him mighty hard . . .'

'Get on with the message, Hal!'

'Oh, yeah — Well, he went to fill his waterbags at the Brazos well, but it was kinda jammed up so he climbed down to free it up.' Wishart swallowed and ran a tongue around his lips as he looked at the impatient deputy. 'Found a couple bodies floatin' around an' got 'em out — Two men, both shot in the back of the head. Farley knew 'em both, couple US Marshals, Foran and McMurphy.'

Brett tightened his lips, spoke only half-aloud. 'Bannerman must've had some pards waiting close by and they jumped 'em along the trail, then brought their bodies back to hide 'em in the well.'

He frowned when Wishart shook his head. 'Been runnin' the keys hot with my opposite number at Fort La Union where Farley took the bodies . . . The army doc says they been dead for a week or more . . . So looks to me, young feller, like you went an' handed Bannerman over to the wrong men!'

3

Manhunter

It was all too simple to figure out.

The men who had posed as Foran and McMurphy had had the telegraph operator at lonely Briscoe Siding send the wires to Las Cruces that changed the arrangements for the handing over of Gil Bannerman.

Then they had shot the operator and the railroad man, burned the place to make it look like Indians had done it. They might have even run off a few cows from nearby ranches to bolster the Indian renegades idea.

Then they had intercepted the real marshals who, coming by horseback, would have naturally stopped at Brazos Station as most travellers did when using that trail. They'd bushwhacked them, dumped their bodies after taking badges and papers and waited for Brett to deliver Bannerman to them . . .

'You're mighty lucky they never just put a bullet in the back of your head and dumped you down that well, too,' opined Morg Blackman. He had turned into a hard-eyed, sour man since the news, seeing his chance at getting his hands on retirement money flying out the window. It was clear he blamed Brett.

'I've been thinking about that,' the deputy admitted. 'I think they went through with that act of exchanging transfer papers and so on to give them time to disappear. If they'd killed me, you'd have wondered why I hadn't returned and likely wired Fort La Union to send some men across to Brazos Station. Letting me come back here made it seem all legitimate and they had a couple extra days to lose themselves in that country.'

Morg Blackman kicked at the scarred leg of his desk. 'Goddamnit, they stole him from under our noses, Caleb! No!

From under *your* nose.'

Brett snapped his gaze to the sheriff's angry face. 'I should've checked that train timetable earlier,' he admitted. 'And I should've figured they wouldn't need two pack-horses of supplies just to ride to Briscoe Siding . . . Yeah, it was my fault we lost him, Morg. I'm sorry.'

'Sorry don't do a helluva lot of good, does it!' Blackman paced restlessly, licking his lips, casting a glance through the open office door towards the *La Bella* across the street and half a block down. 'We've lost the reward money, damnit! That was my retirement! I was countin' on that, Caleb, you know that . . . Hell, to work so damn hard, to have him *here*, in our own jail and then . . . '

He threw up his hands, grabbed down his hat from the wall peg. 'I'm gonna get drunk!'

'That'll help bring him back,' allowed Brett and he was surprised at the twisted hate on the old sheriff's face as the man paused briefly in the doorway.

'You lost him. *You* bring him back!'

Then he stormed across the street and Brett tightened his lips as he reached for his tobacco sack and papers.

Yeah. He intended to bring back Gil Bannerman, all right. Morg was right: it had been his fault.

Now it was up to him to correct his mistake . . .

★ ★ ★

Rose was pale and tight-faced when he went around to the rented cottage for his supper as usual and to tell her he would be starting out to hunt for Bannerman the next day.

'Damn you, Caleb Brett!' she greeted him at the door and stomped away down the short hallway to the parlour.

He followed slowly, removing his hat, running fingers through his sweat-tousled dark hair. He paused in the doorway. She was kneeling beside a sofa, holding a damp cloth to her father's face. The sheriff snored and moaned in a drunken sleep. Brett could smell vomit and saw rags and a tin bowl pushed under one end of the sofa. Morg's shirt was stained.

'Hell, Rose, why didn' you send for me?' He started forward but stopped at the look on her face.

'Send for you? What would be the use! You did this to him!' There were tears filling her eyes.

'He did it to himself, Rose. While I've been arranging things for a manhunt all afternoon, Morg's contribution was to swill booze in the *La Bella*.'

'You know he's weak! And he's getting old — He — he *needed* that reward money! It was his only chance — He hasn't been able to save anything since Mama died . . . '

'I can believe that.'

She stood up abruptly, hands on hips, eyes blazing. 'And what does that mean?'

He was about to retort, but cooled down abruptly, making a meaningless gesture with his hat. 'Forget it, Rose — I'm leaving tomorrow to try to pick up Bannerman's trail.'

'I thought you would have been gone by now!'

He had seen her before when she was mad and it always bewildered him that such a passive, loving woman as Rose could be — and *was* most of the time — could turn into the cold-eyed, unfeeling witch she became when something occasionally really upset her. Thinking back, it was usually something to do with her father . . .

'Yeah, well, I just wanted to let you know,' he said quietly. 'You can tell Morg when he comes around . . . And you'd do well to keep him away from the saloon, Rose.'

'Good night, Caleb!' she said coldly. 'I'm sure you can find your own way out!'

He hesitated. 'Tell Morg I've hired

young Ben Tully — he's a good tracker and a fine shot.'

'And if you bring Bannerman in, *he'll* want a share of the reward!'

'God — *damn* the reward, Rose! In any case, Ben'll be entitled to it . . . ' He paused at the door, looking at her pinched face. 'Morg can have my share — It looks as if I won't be needing it.'

It was only after she heard the front door slam behind him that she realized he had meant it seemed as if they wouldn't be getting married now.

The tears suddenly rolled down her face and she sobbed quietly into her apron, sniffing, and looking down at her father.

'Oh, Dad! Why do you have to be such a — problem!'

★ ★ ★

Gil Bannerman sat with his back propped up against his saddle, cleaning his guns. He had already done the rifle and was replacing the cylinder in his six-gun, concentrating on the job. Most of the other outlaws in Heck Coburn's group never touched their guns except to use them or reload. Only when they were deeply fouled with powder residue did they take the trouble to disassemble them and drop them into a bucket of lye or soapy water.

But Bannerman had lived by the gun for many years and more than once a well-oiled and cleaned weapon had been the means of saving his neck.

Coburn, the man who had posed as Marshal Marv Foran at Brazos Station, stood up from where he sat on a log near the campfire and walked across, dropping to the ground beside Bannerman.

'Gabe's still a mess,' he said.

Bannerman didn't look up from his gun, fingers manipulating screws and wedges expertly as he reassembled the weapon. 'Lucky the sonuver's still alive.'

'Man, he had to make it look good!'

Now Bannerman glanced up and turned his face so Coburn could see the bruised swelling on the side of his head where Gabe Blanchard, the man who had posed as Marshal McMurphy, had hit him with his shotgun butt. 'He made it look good, all right. Still, can't see proper outta my left eye and head's throbbin' like an Apache war drum.'

Heck Coburn sighed as he twisted up a cigarette. 'Yeah, I guess he got a mite enthusiastic, but what you done to him, Gil . . . '

Bannerman smiled thinly as he recalled that moment when they had stopped in a dry wash and taken off his manacles and shackles. Brett was long gone and there was no need for the charade any longer, although Bannerman had demanded to know why they hadn't simply shot down the deputy at the old stage station.

'He'll take a couple of days to get back to Las Cruces,' Coburn had explained. 'We'll lose ourselves in those two days. Could be a week or more after that before they figure we weren't the real marshals . . . '

'Yeah, well I want Brett nailed — and I aim to do it,' Bannerman had gritted, rubbing circulation back into his wrists and legs. Then he had stood tentatively, found he could stand firmly and said, 'But first . . . '

He moved quickly, stumbling a little, but taking Gabe Blanchard by surprise as he grabbed the man's boot and heaved him out of the saddle. Blanchard, being a big, heavy man, hit hard and lay there dazed briefly — long enough for Bannerman to snatch the double-barrelled Greener from the saddle scabbard. When Blanchard saw the move his eyes widened and he started to fight to a sitting position, groping for his six-gun.

Bannerman kicked him in the chest, knocking him backwards. Coburn yelled but one look from Bannerman and he stayed put. Then the shotgun's barrels slammed across Blanchard's head, sending him sprawling on his side. Bannerman's boots thudded into the big belly and ribs, bounced off the man's head, crushed his nose and mouth. Blanchard was well out of it and still Bannerman kept kicking, finally driving the steel-shod butt of the shotgun between his eyes.

Coburn pursed his lips thoughtfully as he looked down at his bloody-faced companion. 'Sure glad it wasn't me hit you . . . Hope you ain't put him outta commission altogether, Gil — We need him for that job we got planned.'

'If he can't ride with us, he don't earn a share. Simple as that, Heck.'

Now it was three days later and big Gabe was still abed, nursing what he claimed were busted ribs. Certainly his nose was smashed and he was missing three front teeth, his mouth puffed and misshapen. One eye was closed and he complained of nausea. Coburn figured it was concussion and all the man needed was rest, but he was a mite concerned about the slow rate of recovery. He had come to depend on Blanchard a lot . . .

'Time's drawin' closer for the job, Gil, and still Gabe ain't movin' around.'

Bannerman tightened a final screw on his six-gun, worked the action, squirted in a couple of drops of oil and then thumbed fresh cartridges into the cylinder's chambers.

'He rides or he don't get paid — I already told you.'

'Yeah, me an' Gabe've been pards for a long time, Gil. You might've had a gripe with him but — well, he's been in on the plannin' right from the start. I figure he's already earned a share.'

Bannerman glanced up, his eyes bleak. 'Long as it comes outta yours. I ain't contributin' a thing unless he takes part. Savvy?'

Coburn nodded, decided to change the subject. 'What about this Brett? You said you were gonna nail him before you did anythin' else . . . '

Bannerman smiled faintly. 'Been

61

thinkin' on it. Don't want him bush-whacked: a bullet's too quick. But I've got me some notion how to wreck the sonuver's life for him before I finish him off — Them few days in Las Cruces hoosegow I picked me a little information I figure I can use ... I'll need one of your men. One that's not well known and can ride around more or less free. Fact, you might be about right, Heck — You ain't wanted in New Mexico are you?'

Coburn was mighty wary now as he shook his head slowly.

'Now I got a lotta things to do, Gil ... '

'Yeah, you have — I'll tell you about 'em.'

He outlined his plan but Coburn shook his head adamantly,

'Uh-uh. Not me, Gil ... But I've got a better idea ... '

★ ★ ★

Ben Tully was a young man in his mid-twenties, some five or six years younger than Caleb Brett. But he was married and responsible, starting a small ranch just outside of town. In fact, it had been Tully's early success that had decided Brett to buy *his* section a bit farther out amongst the foothills, although he had had to borrow heavily to do it. Then Rose's insistence that she wanted a fully finished house before the wedding had put him deeper into debt when he had approached the lumber mill for dressed timber to line and partition the cabin. He didn't blame Rose: it wouldn't have been much fun for a girl who had lived in towns most of her life to suddenly have to make a new life in a draughty, rough-hewn log cabin . . .

But Brett tried to push these thoughts from him now as he and Ben Tully rode warily through the Sacramento Hills. Tully had grown up in these parts and had also served time as an Indian scout with the army at Fort La

Union to make a few extra dollars. He was a fine tracker, a crack-shot, and he had plenty of guts.

Brett had hired him at a dollar a day — out of county funds . . . but there was an understanding that Ben would share in any reward forthcoming if they captured Bannerman again.

Tully had a face that made him look a mite older than he was, but when he smiled it was transformed into that of a man who was still very much a boy at heart.

'I don't think they'd've come back here,' Brett said as they rode down out of the high pass. 'They were heading south-east when I watched them ride away from the Brazos Station. Not that that means much, I guess, but I reckon Bannerman would stay in Texas. He knows that neck of the woods best.'

'You didn't recognize the men who said they were marshals?'

Brett scowled. 'I thought mebbe Foran looked vaguely familiar but once they came up with their badge numbers and the right process papers, I had to tell myself they were who they claimed . . . which is a long way round of saying, no, I didn't recognize either man . . . But then, I don't know any of Bannerman's gang.'

Tully nodded. 'Guess the marshals will have men out looking, too.'

'Yeah — there was a wire came, wanting me to stay put in Las Cruces while they sent a man down to investigate, but the hell with that. I can be looking for Bannerman instead of sitting around on my hands waiting to answer a lot of questions.'

Tully looked at him sharply. 'They're not blamin' you, are they?'

Brett laughed shortly. 'Everyone's blaming me, Ben — rightly so, I guess. The only way I can square things is to bring in Bannerman again.'

Tully smiled that boyish smile of his. 'Don't worry, Caleb — We'll do it. We'll track down that killer and drag him back at the end of a rope.'

Brett smiled. He hoped Tully was

right — otherwise he would be finished as a lawman.

He felt he was already finished as a would-be husband . . .

They crossed the state line before sundown and Brett immediately began looking for tracks. Tully kept riding and they made a cold camp in a redwalled canyon that had a shallow stream flowing through it. Tully had brought him here, telling him it was south-east of Brazos Station and would be a good place for the fake marshals to have stopped and set Bannerman free of his shackles and manacles.

After seeing the place, Brett agreed and when he awoke he found that Tully's bedroll was already empty and the man's horse was missing. He started the breakfast fire and had the meal about cooked when Tully rode in on his roan, rifle in hand. He dismounted, crossed to squat beside Brett who was juggling the iron skillet over the flames. The last of their bacon sizzled amidst beans and stale cornpone now frying in the grease.

'Smells good,' opined Tully.

'You earn your breakfast?' Brett asked and Tully nodded slowly.

'Found tracks across the stream. Three riders, two pack-horses, best part of ten days old I'd reckon.'

'Could be our men,' Brett allowed, dishing out food onto two tin plates and handing one to Tully with a fork. He picked up the other and began to eat slowly.

'There was some sort of scuffle or fight by the sign.'

Brett frowned. 'Don't sound right.'

'Sign's there . . . But they all rode on together. I went as far as the end of the canyon and it drops away in a slope of loose scree. No more tracks. But might be below in the brush.'

So they hurried through breakfast, rolled smokes but didn't light them until they were mounted and riding out of the red-walled canyon.

Tully picked up signs of a trail but

there had been an effort made to cover it up. He lost it beyond the foothill where the timber thickened and at a point where one direction was just about as good as another. There was the railroad north and east, Jumping Man Springs to the south, the trail to El Paso south and west. All were well-used trails and showed no tracks that Tully could match to those seen in the canyon with the red walls.

Brett sat his bay, heel hooked on the saddlehorn, staring up into the heavy timber of the ridges due north.

'You know that country up there?'

'Know enough to stay clear of it,' Ben Tully said. 'Renegade Apaches use it a lot, also whites on the dodge . . . ' He stopped abruptly, his gaze sharpening. 'Yeah! Couple of outlaw outfits use them ridges — Moss Garnett's bunch for one . . . They call it Midnight Ridge.'

'I never heard of Garnett hooking up with Bannerman.'

'Well, he rode with him at least

once — on the Wichita Falls raid when they took both banks in the town on the same mornin'. You must've heard about that.'

'Who hasn't? Didn't know Bannerman was in on it, though.'

'Oh, yeah, sure thing — He was the one killed the manager of one bank and the bullet went clear through and crippled a clerk standin' behind him. As the manager fell he lurched into Bannerman and dragged off his mask. The clerk lay doggo and positively identified Bannerman later — I was with the army at the time and the posse borrowed us scouts to help track down the robbers. We lost 'em in these ridges but caught one man who'd been wounded durin' the raid. The others'd left him for dead but he lived long enough to tell us it was Moss Garnett . . . '

Brett looked steadily at the young tracker. 'Feel like heading in there?'

'Well, I can think of other things I'd rather be doin', but you hired me,

Caleb. You point where you want me to go and I'll go.'

Brett smiled faintly as he jerked his head towards the heavily timbered ridge.

'That's where we're headed.'

★ ★ ★

They were ready to give up when the second sundown came without any sign of Moss Garnett or anyone else using the dark, secret trails on Midnight Ridge.

But then Brett woke during the night and saw a dark figure hunched over the grubsack, barely visible in the glow of the dying embers. The deputy whipped up his six-gun and the man leapt upright and started to run the moment the hammer began to ratchet back to full cock. He had only taken three steps when Tully jabbed his rifle barrel between the man's lower legs and sent him sprawling. Before he could recover, Tully was upon him, driving the rifle butt against the intruder's head.

He dragged him back to the small fire that Brett was now building up from the embers. 'We got us an Injun. Apache — and half-starved by the looks of him.'

The Apache was skinny, his ribs and bones showing through a thin layer of sinew and muscle. He wasn't very old, maybe just into warriorhood a couple of years. His weapons were a wired-up Spencer carbine with a wobbly side hammer that must have made shooting mighty uncertain, and a wooden-handled knife in a rawhide sheath. He smelled of the wild and had a small medicine bag dangling around his neck on a thong. His breechclout was filthy and ragged.

'Not the best specimen of your noble savage,' opined Brett, seeing the barely contained fear in the man's eyes. Tully had bound his arms behind him, using rawhide tie-thongs around the bony elbows. He made the Indian kneel by the fire.

'You know any Apache?' Brett asked Tully and when the tracker said he could speak some Mimbre Brett signed for him to question the prisoner.

Tully did so but the Indian didn't answer until the tracker smacked him hard across the face with his open hand. Then he spoke sullenly, voice hoarse with hunger.

'He was with a small band who live in these hills, hittin' the small ranchers from time to time. But some white men jumped 'em, shot and scalped his friends. He doesn't say how he got away — He's scared because he thinks we're pards of the killers. Garnett's bunch.'

'Let him think that. Ask him does he know where these white men hole up . . . Tell him if he talks true, I'll give him a sack of grub. And some coffee. Let him think we're lost.'

Tully frowned. 'Ain't no need for the bribe, Caleb! We got him cold and he's hungry enough to talk his head off.'

'Make him the offer. I've never seen

a more starved-looking Apache still walking around.'

Tully seemed reluctant but shortly the Indian nodded and spoke for half a minute in his guttural language.

'Hell, Caleb! Put out that fire, man! We're practically within spittin'-distance of Moss Garnett's hideout!'

Brett went back on his promise to the Apache to the extent that he insisted the man show them where Garnett's hideout was before handing over the sack of food.

The man was leery but led the way through timber and over an outcrop of rugged rocks before stopping and pointing to the base of a sheer wall where bushes grew thickly. He made signs with his hands that the bushes could be parted and would lead them to the outlaws' hideout. He said something to Tully.

'What was that?' Brett asked.

'Says there's only three men there — That's why he thought we were the other two returning to the camp,

73

figured we'd gone to get supplies and to sell the scalps.'

Brett thrust out the grubsack and the Indian hesitated, looked deeply into the deputy's face, then snatched the sack and a moment later was gone.

Brett blinked. 'Well, I never believed in ghosts till now . . . '

Tully worked the lever on his rifle silently, lowered the hammer gently. Brett carried his carbine.

They were afoot, figuring this was the best and most silent way to go into the outlaw camp.

'We goin'in?' asked Tully softly, parting the bushes enough to show the dark shape of a narrow tunnel thrugh the rock.

'That's what we came for, Ben . . . '

Caleb Brett levered a shell into his carbine's breech, thrust past the tracker and, crouching, made his way into the tunnel.

4

Scalp Hunters

The tunnel roof was lower than they expected and both men swore softly as they bumped their heads, even though bent over. Brett wondered how Garnett and his bounty hunters had gotten their mounts through here.

But it was short and brought them out onto a long, shallow slope that led down into a small grassy canyon. Pausing to stare around, silhouetting the walls as well as he could against the stars, Brett whispered to Ben Tully. 'Looks like the walls don't meet far as I can make out. Could mean there's another way out.'

'Reckon there would be — That tunnel's too low for horses.'

Brett nodded. 'OK — Can you see that pale patch on the wall where it hooks to the right? Just below it there looks to be a campfire. Can't see it but there's something wavering out there. Could be smoke or even heat.'

Tully sniffed. 'Woodsmoke all right. You want I should make my way around beyond the camp — if that's what it is?'

'Yeah, do that. I'll give you ten minutes, then I'll make my way down. If they are camped there, we go in on my signal — which will be the first shot. So you'll have to be ready.'

'I'll be there in five.'

'Make it ten and be sure.'

Tully's teeth showed faintly as he smiled and made his way quickly down the long slope. Brett watched until he dropped from sight behind some brush and then started down, angling to the left of Tully. The grass smelled sweet on the canyon floor and was springy underfoot. Well watered, he thought, and looked around for the stream.

He couldn't hear any water flowing over stones or gravel but came to a narrow creek, moving sluggishly over sand. It was just too wide to leap so he waded across silently, crouched by a deadfall on the far bank. He could smell grease and the odour of cooked bacon now, as well as coffee and woodsmoke. Easing around the deadfall, he came to a patch of grass with three hobbled horses grazing on it. He almost blundered into the animals and one lifted its head, ears pricked, whinnied low. He reached out and gently ran a hand down the tensed neck muscles. He stroked until he felt them relax, murmured quietly to the horse and made his way around the animals.

Beyond he saw the red glow of the burned-down campfire, straining to find the men. Three of them, snoring and grunting in their blanket rolls, all on the far side to where he stood.

He judged Tully ought to be in position by now although he couldn't see him, notched back the carbine's hammer and drew bead on the embers.

His first shot sent the coals erupting like a firework and the speed with which the trio came out of their blankets, guns blazing, took him by surprise.

These were men who hunted Apaches for the bounty on their scalps: he ought to have figured they would sleep mighty light. Likely they had heard that horse whinny and had lain doggo, waiting to see who was moving about their hidden canyon.

A slug clipped his hat and dust spurted and he fumbled the levering of the fresh shell into his carbine's breech. He had to jack it again to clear it and by then bullets were cutting the air close to his face. One kicked dirt against his cheek as he dropped flat, triggered and rolled, levering as he did so. When he flopped onto his belly he fired again at a gun flash, and then realized the whole night seemed to be torn apart by gun flashes. The stabs of powder flame lit a small camp site, showed brush and rock, maybe part of a wall. The guns hammered constantly, sweeping around now. He hoped those gun flashes off to one side meant Tully was shooting into the camp.

Then he wrenched around on his belly, dropping his carbine, palming up his Peacemaker. He drove four shots into the line of flashes across the remains of the fire, put his left hand down on a hot coal and yelped as he flung himself back . . . an instant before lead tore into the turf, right beneath his body. He rolled again, hammered two more shots, realizing only after he's fired that there was only one gun shooting at him now. The one he figured was Tully's cracked twice more in the echoing whiplash of the rifle and then the fading drumming of the gunfire was the only sound in the canyon.

Except for Brett's breath as it hissed through flared nostrils.

'Caleb?' a voice called softly.

'Here.' He rolled quickly as he spoke — his ears were ringing and although he thought it was Tully's voice, he couldn't be sure.

Then a man moaned, sobbed in agony.

'One of 'em's still alive,' Tully opined quietly.

'That don't make him lucky,' Brett said, taking a chance now and standing, ramming out the used shells and reloading his Peacemaker swiftly.

Ben Tully came down from beyond the brush, where Brett had seen his rifle flashes. Brett dragged some of the scattered coals together and dropped some kindling on, stepping back as it flared, staying out of the light. Tully kept to the shadows, too, moving about amongst the sprawled men.

'These two are finished — Must be the one near you, Caleb.'

Brett looked at the man, saw him move, trying to push off his side onto his back. He grunted with the effort and flopped back. Brett knelt beside him, hot gun muzzle pressing against the wounded man's forehead as he thumbed back his hammer.

'Well, Ben, if this hombre didn't have a beard, I'd say he looks tolerably like Moss Garnett. You seen that dodger we got in the office at Las Cruces?'

Ben came up, standing over the wounded outlaw, kicking a little more kindling onto the fire. As it flared he nodded and prodded the man with his rifle barrel.

'Yep, that's old Moss, all right . . . You're lookin' old, pardner. Oughta shave that beard.'

Garnett flicked pain-filled eyes from one man to the other. He swore, pressing both hands into his left side, low down. 'Hell, I thought it was at least a troop of rangers, marshals, anyways. Don't tell me I've been took by a coupla hick lawmen, not even from Texas!'

'Guess you'll just have to live with it, Moss — Though wouldn't reckon that'll be for long. You're gut-shot.'

'Yeah, you bastard! You done it! With

81

your second goddamn shot . . . Wouldn't care if I'da got you first but . . . ' Pain hit him hard and he gritted his teeth, trying to hold in the agonized cry. His teeth drew blood from his bottom lip before he slumped. 'Finish me!' he gasped.

'Not yet,' Brett said, examining the bullet hole through the crown of his hat. 'Need you to talk, Moss.'

'Christ, wish it didn't hurt so much to — laugh!'

Suddenly he screamed and convulsed and Brett swore as he saw Tully had caused it by poking his rifle muzzle into the outlaw's wound and corkscrewing it brutally, the foresight reaming the bleeding hole.

'The hell're you doing!' Brett said, jumping up but the young tracker was looking down at the writhing, sobbing Garnett. He planted a boot on the man's chest.

'You damn scalp hunters make me sick to my belly! I seen whole Injun villages of women and kids and old folk, all scalped by the likes of you . . . Take 'em on down to Mexico and sell 'em there, don't you? Twenty-five for kids, fifty for women, hundred pesos for men! Not often we found any real warriors you'd scalped — They were likely to fight back, weren't they? You're scum, Garnett! Cesspool *scum*!'

He kicked the outlaw in the side, lifting him a foot along the ground towards the fire before Brett could push him back. 'Take it easy, Ben!'

Tully's eyes were wild in the firelight. 'You ever seen the handiwork of snakes like this?'

Brett nodded. 'Not kids, but women and old folk. Once . . . we thought it was an enemy tribe but turned out to be white scalp hunters . . . But you'll kill him this way, Ben.'

'Yeah — and he'll feel plenty before I finally finish him.' Tully drew his hunting knife. 'When I was scoutin' if we caught up with bounty hunters like Garnett and left any of 'em alive, we took their scalps . . . '

'Jesus! Stop him, Brett!' Garnett screamed as Tully knelt and twisted his fingers in the man's greasy hair. '*Stop him*! . . . I'll tell you whatever — you wanna — know . . . '

Tully retained his grip, knife edge against the man's hairline. At a nod from Brett he asked, 'Where'll we find Gil Bannerman?'

The surprise on Garnett's face was evident even through pain. 'Banner — ? Hell, he ain't here. He's with Heck — Heck Coburn.'

'Where?' The knife edge drew blood and a thin ribbon trickled through the sweat beads on Garnett's forehead. He moaned in fear.

'I — dunno! Gospel! — Look, Heck's gotta gal in Jumpin' Man Springs — Sherry someone — He spends a deal of time with her. She . . . Aw, Judas! The pain!' One clawed hand grabbed Tully's rigid forearm. 'Help me! Finish me — off! I — I dunno nothin' else — Heck's plannin' somethin' big, that's all I hear — it's why he needed — Bannerman . . . '

He drew up his knees, thrashing wildly and screaming, and for a moment Brett thought Tully had started to scalp the man but Ben jumped back, startled.

It was a spasm of severe pain that had wrenched at the outlaw and Brett took a quick bead, put a bullet through his head and he sagged back limply.

Tully sighed. 'We might've gotten more outta him.'

Then he turned away quickly and Brett heard him being sick on the other side of the line of brush.

He smiled faintly: he was glad young Ben wasn't quite as hard as he'd tried to make out.

Never hurt any man to have a little softness in him.

★ ★ ★

To reach Jumping Man Springs, they had to circle Red Bluff Lake and ride almost as far as the Prairie Dog Creek fork of the alkaline Toyah Creek.

It was a trailtown stopover now for herds of the south-west on their way to El Paso. So there were a couple of saloons, a cathouse, some stores and a livery, a stage depot, and a few scattered houses set in the middle of a grassy plain that stretched horizon-wards in every direction but west. There the bleached monotony was broken by scattered trees and brush, a few low hogbacks and one spine of craggy mountains towards the Diablo Sierras.

'Them mountains are s'posed to hide more outlaws than the Indian Territory,' Ben Tully said as they approached the town from the south, having skirted it in the dark to make their approach from this side.

It would fit their planned story of being a couple of drifters looking for trail work, coming up from that direction.

'You reckon Heck Coburn's hideout is up there?' asked Brett.

Tully shrugged. 'He's gotta be some-wheres close if he visits a gal in the Springs.'

Brett nodded. 'You might have something there, Ben. But let's see if we can find the gal first. She might lead us to Coburn if nothing else.'

'Er — I ain't a lot of good when it comes to makin' women talk, Caleb.' Ben sounded embarrassed.

Brett smiled. 'Me neither, but let's see what kinda gal she is.'

They found out within minutes of hitting the first bar in Jumping Man Springs.

'Sherry West?' the barkeep said in answer to Brett's casual query.

'Sherry something. Could be West.'

'Only Sherry we got in town.' He winked at a couple of dusty trailhands hunched over their drinks a couple of feet away. 'Just as well, too, eh, boys, goin' by the looks of you.'

The trailhands, tough-looking and rugged, surprisingly reddened and dropped their heads a little sheepishly.

Brett and Tully were puzzled but the barkeep grinned, showing worn, mossy teeth.

'Sherry runs the cathouse,' he explained. 'Once in a while, if a customer can come up with the ante — she'll accommodate 'em.' He shook his head wonderingly. 'She's kind of a legend in these parts — not that I've been lucky enough to make the grade but these boys were flush last night and now I'm standin' 'em a farewell drink before they drag ass outta here — and they reckon it was worth every cent. Am I right, boys?'

'So long,' growled one man downing his drink. 'And I'd put a button on that lip, feller.'

His companion wasn't so grouchy. He smiled and hitched at his gunbelt. 'Man, I hate trail-drivin', but I'm gonna sign up with the biggest, longest trail herd that's goin' — just so's I can get enough to come back an' see ol' Sherry one more time before I die.'

The barkeep was pleased and watched

them fondly as they walked out. Then he critically examined Brett and Tully.

'You fellers'd stand a chance — specially him.' He gestured to Ben. 'She likes 'em young.'

Brett arched his eyebrows at Tully and downed his beer. 'Well, let's go — This Sherry sounds like the kinda gal I been waitin' to meet.'

'Tell 'er Mick sent ya!' the 'keep called as they headed for the batwings. When they had gone through, the two 'trailhands' who had left looking so bedraggled and weary slipped in the side door and hurried to the bar where Mick was pouring them two free drinks for their cooperation. He poured a third for himself and lifted it in salute.

'I surely do enjoy a good joke! Here's to many more, fellers!'

★ ★ ★

The place Mick had directed Brett and Tully to was called Sherry's Ace-in-the-Hole and was one block down and one street over from the saloon. They thought it looked more like a gambling house than a girlie-parlour but figured this was just the front.

It was adobe with upper and lower levels joined by a rickety-looking outside stairway. The lawmen took time for a good look around, marking likely places for escape or hiding if need be before pushing through the chipped batwings. They found themselves in a small bar-cum-parlour separated from another room by an archway through which they could see gaming tables, well patronized, the players tended by painted women, all beneath a heavy pall of tobacco smoke. Cones of light from hanging lanterns spilled onto the tables.

'Cathouse must be upstairs,' opined Ben Tully as Brett ordered two beers. The barkeep with the hostile eyes told them that house whiskey was the only drink served here. He flexed bulging muscles against the rolled-up sleeves of his grimy shirt and looked challenging as he set up two shot-glasses of amber-coloured liquid. Brett sniffed and asked for water and it seemed a great effort for the big man to reach beneath the counter for a terracotta jug of murky water. It was highly alkaline and did little to cut the bite of the rotgut whiskey. Brett's lips stung from his first sip and Tully winced at the sulphurous smell and pushed the glass away.

'Somethin' wrong with our hooch?' the barman demanded.

'Not if you've got a cast-iron belly,' Brett answered. 'Even then I wouldn't take any bets it wouldn't burn clear through your boots.'

The barkeep jerked his head towards the archway. 'You don't want a drink, through there's the gamblin' — Play your cards right you might even be lucky enough to find an accommodatin' lady, but that's strictly between you an' her — If that don't suit . . . ' He swivelled his hard, flint-like eyes towards the batwings.

'Matter of fact we are looking for a

gal,' Brett said, toying with the glass of acidic whiskey. 'Name of Sherry — We were told she can drive a man all the way to heaven and back. For the right price.'

Brett didn't think it possible, but the barkeep's face hardened even more. He studied both men, tapping thick, blunt fingers against the counter-top. 'Mick sent you, huh?' At Brett's surprised nod the man's mouth tightened. 'That son of a bitch! I warned him about his stupid jokes . . . Now you two get the hell outta here while you can still walk!'

'Hey, you ain't real friendly, are you!' hissed Tully.

'Not paid to be friendly. Paid to head off trouble — I got back-up I can call on, too.' He looked at Tully insultingly. 'In your case, I reckon I won't need it.'

'OK,' cut in Brett quickly, seeing Ben's mouth tightening. 'We've been had — but we'd still like to see this Sherry.'

'By God, you're just out for trouble, ain't you?'

Brett laid a silver dollar on the bar and the man sneered, picked up a glass and began polishing, ignoring the coin. Brett laid a gold five-dollar piece alongside and suddenly the man set down the glass, facing them, and when he removed his polishing cloth the money had disappeared. He leaned on one elbow, said in a whisper, 'She's outta town.'

'When'll she be back, goddamnit?' snapped Ben impatiently but Brett frowned and shook his head.

'I — don't — know,' the barkeep said flatly and clearly. 'Now, vamoose, before I change my mind and call the help.'

'Like Heck Coburn, maybe?' Brett asked softly. 'I hear she's his woman.'

That did it.

The barkeep stiffened then slapped a big, raw-knuckled hand flatly on the counter-top, leaning forward a little, nostrils flaring.

'The hell're you doin' now?' demanded Ben Tully, ready and eager for trouble, sick of this tough, hostile man who seemed intent on prodding them into some kind of fool play even though Mick had set them up for a joke.

The barkeep sniffed loudly. 'I'm gettin' me a whiff of 'law' and it ain't no jailhouse stink!'

While he spoke he moved quickly, catching the lawmen unawares as he whipped up a sawed-off shotgun from under the counter. Other drinkers scattered. One of the waitresses who had been watching from the archway screamed and suddenly ran back into the other room. Her scream caused confusion and chaos in seconds and then the grim-faced barkeep had his hammers thumbed back, covering Brett and Tully.

'What the hell you after, you sons of bitches? You tryin' to get a line on Heck?'

Tully licked his lips, looked at Brett who hadn't taken his eyes off the shotgun, although he spread his hands slightly out from his sides in a token lifting.

'Looking for Gil Bannerman if you want the gospel of it,' he said flatly and the barman blinked, startled by such an admission. Only the foolish or the fearless would say such a thing. The slow crooked smile started to spread across his face and Brett's gaze travelled past the man's thick shoulders to the running people in the room beyond.

'By God, Ben! There he is!' he snapped suddenly and Tully jumped, startled, which in turn startled the barkeep and the man snapped his head around before he could stop himself.

When he looked back — in a fraction of a second — he saw Brett's sixgun blurring out of leather as the deputy thrust Tully to one side. Brett went the other way, throwing himself bodily sideways, shooting in mid-air as the sawed-off thundered, its charge of shot gouging the adobe wall, splintering a table, sending patrons diving under the batwings. Brett hit on his right shoulder, rolled and came thrusting up to his knees, slapping at the hammer spur with the edge of his left hand. The two bullets struck the wide-chested barman high up, hurling him into the rows of bottles and glasses. The man dropped to his knees, eyes wide and bulging in shock as the smoking shotgun spilled from his grip.

Tully yelled and Brett spun that way, seeing the young tracker on one knee, shooting at two hard-bitten men charging through the archway, guns blazing in their big fists. One man went down hard, yelling and cursing as he clasped a shattered hip. The second man twisted as he grabbed at his shoulder, slammed into the archway support and tried to lift his gun. But it fell from his grasp and he looked scared as he tried to thrust his free, bloodied hand high.

On the floor above, women could be heard crying out to each other.

Men swore, but no one else seemed interested in buying in to the fight.

Brett went around the bar, stepping over a couple of prone patrons, and saw the barkeep sprawled amongst the slops and broken glass, one hand thrust into his chest wounds, face already grey, eyes dulling. Brett shook his shoulder but the man was too far gone.

He straightened, walked across to the man with the shoulder wound hunched in the archway covered by Tully. The man with the shattered hip writhed on the floor, on the verge of passing out with the pain. Brett pressed his hot Peacemaker's muzzle against the other man's head, cocked the hammer.

'Looks like it's up to you, amigo.'

'Wh — what? Man, I'm hurtin'!'

'Not as much as you could be — All we want to know is where Sherry's gone.'

The man, shaking and white now, blood dripping from the fingers of his useless arm, looked from one man to the other. 'That's — all . . . ?'

'And anything else you'd care to contribute,' Brett told him, smiling coldly.

The man ran a tongue over his lips, grimacing and swaying as he held his throbbing shoulder. 'Look, all I know is, Heck Coburn come in here late last night . . . He . . . he hauled me outta bed an' told me to get up and carry Sherry's carpetbag across to the stage depot.'

Brett frowned. 'Middle of the night?'

'Sure — stages come through at all hours now, trying to make the connection with the railroad . . . '

'All right. You took her luggage to the stage depot. Where'd she buy a ticket for?'

The man suddenly swayed and Brett steadied him but he felt the man's legs give way and let him slide down to his knees.

'Amigo, you're likely not just actin' up right now, but I'd want to be sure so if you pass out before you tell me what I want to know, you're gonna wish you hadn't tried to fool me.'

The man croaked, 'Las Cruces — Heck sent her to — Las Cruces . . . Somethin' to do with a hombre name of — Brett . . .'

Then he fell flat on his face.

5

Outlaw Country

There was no telegraph station in Jumping Man Springs so they rode out to Van Horn and sent a wire to Morg Blackman. It asked him to find and hold Sherry West — a rough description given to Brett by the wounded man was added.

The message finished with; *May be wearing blonde wig, using false name. Love to Rose* . . .

He hesitated about adding that last and Ben Tully, watching him scrawl out the message, looked at him with puzzlement.

'Countin' the pennies or you got yourself a leetle woman trouble, Caleb?'

Brett smiled thinly. 'Just a leetle, Ben . . . Leastways, I hope that's all it is.'

He didn't elaborate and stayed while

the operator sent the message.

Outside in the battering heat of the sun, the glare from the adobe town causing them to squint, Ben hitched at his gunbelt, hefting his rifle before cradling it across his chest, held in the crook of his left arm.

'Where to?' He arched his eyebrows and nodded towards the distant Diablo Sierras. 'Thataway?'

Brett looked thoughtful, rolling a cigarette and handing the makings to Tully. They lit up and smoked in the shade offered by a brush awning outside a barber's shop and the cigarettes were burned half way down before Caleb Brett answered.

'I've got me a hunch that Heck Coburn's hanging out up there and if he's there so's Bannerman — and the rest of Coburn's gang. You figure you and me'd be a match for a bunch like that?'

Tully drew on his cigarette, exhaled smoke through his nostrils. 'Well — mebbe not, but then again mebbe two men could get in there and stay hidden while they looked around better than a full-blown posse could.'

'Uh-huh, already figured that way — But what happens if we find 'em? We're still only two men. And a full-blown posse would be mighty handy to be able to call on at that stage.'

Tully grinned. 'How come you can always shoot down my notions and do it so blamed well I get mad at *myself* for even suggestin' 'em in the first place?'

Brett laughed. 'Just got a knack of looking at things from all angles — Mostly the one that'll save my hide.'

'Man, you make it sound like you're Cautious Charley and your record of arrests and gunfights kick that notion clear outta the window.'

'It only looks that way, Ben — If I take a risk, it means I figure I've got at least a fifty-fifty chance of walking away from the trouble . . . But there's two of us now, remember? You're a married man and Nancy's expecting her first, so I hear.'

Tully blushed a little. 'Yeah — due about Fall. But, Caleb, you don't have to pussyfoot just because I'm here. I've had my share of danger and I know how to handle myself and don't mind the risks. Specially if there's a chance of pickin' up a fistful of dollars.'

Caleb Brett studied the young tracker. Sure, Ben had never lacked guts. He was a fine young hombre this, clean-cut, lived by an old and honourable code, could shoot straight and would never run out on a pard . . .

But Brett felt a mite uneasy about leading such a man into the Diablos where they might run up against the likes of Coburn and Bannerman. These outlaws were kings of the dungheap down this way. There was little law around except for a handful of rangers or some smalltown sheriffs who would look the other way for the chance of a few extra dollars in their pockets . . .

Coburn and Bannerman could literally

get away with murder in this neck of the woods and had been doing so for a long time now . . .

Brett took a final drag on his cigarette, dropped it to the boardwalk and mashed it under his dusty boot.

'Ben, we'd better stock up on supplies — They tell me there ain't no stores in the Diablos.'

Ben Tully grinned from ear to ear, hefting his rifle.

'*Now* we're in full agreement! Let's go, amigo. I got big plans for my share of the bounty!'

★ ★ ★

Gil Bannerman had just unsaddled his mount after having taken a ride through the rough, razor-back terrain surrounding the hideout — 'Goin' stir-crazy', as he put it, eager to get moving on his and Coburn's big plan.

He turned from the corrals and saw Heck Coburn sitting outside one of the ramshackle cabins beside Gabe

Blanchard, who still sported a couple of black eyes and a deep, bruised gash just above the bridge of his nose.

The man glared at Bannerman hostilely but the big killer ignored him, hunkered down beside Heck Coburn, reached over and whipped the tagged tobacco sack out of the man's shirt pocket. He began to make a thick quirley.

'Country's dry as a rattler's butt,' he commented. 'Not enough foliage on the brush and trees. We're gonna have us a time gettin' away.' Coburn snapped his gaze around sharply and Bannerman fired a vesta on his thumbnail and lit up. 'We'll be seen through the dry brush after we pull off the deal. Reckon we oughta give some thought to another escape route. Trackin' us'll be too easy the way we got planned.'

'Country's all the same this time of year,' opined Gabe Blanchard but flushed and looked away when Bannerman threw him a hard look. 'Well, it is! It ain't rained for weeks! 'Sides, there

105

ain't time to change our plans now, is there, Heck?'

'Not *our* plans, Gabe,' Bannerman replied before Coburn could speak. 'You ain't contributed nothin' to 'em — and I already told Heck, you don't ride on this deal, you don't get a share.'

Blanchard's jaw dropped and he hitched his bulk around towards Coburn. 'Heck . . . ? I'm still sick . . . '

'Don't worry, Gabe, I'll see you right,' Coburn told him without looking at him. He kept his narrowed gaze on Gil Bannerman. 'Kinda late in the day for a change of plan, Gil.'

'You're a long time dead, Heck,' was Bannerman's only comment and after a spell, Coburn stood, went into the hut and returned a few minutes later with the map he had drawn weeks ago and which they had been working from to plan approach and escape routes.

'Only other trail out that we could use is this one here, leads south towards the Rio, and first thing they're gonna do is plug up the border.'

Bannerman scoffed. 'Let 'em. We never planned on crossin' the Rio, anyways.'

'No, but like I said, we don't use the original trail, a run for the border's the only other way out. Unless you want to chance the high pass through to Sierra Blanca. Joe Vardis'd hide us out there — but he'd want a big share.'

Bannerman smiled crookedly. '*I'll* pay him his share — the price of a bullet.'

Heck Coburn stirred restlessly. 'First thing you always want to do is killin' Gil. It won't work — that's Vardis's dunghill and . . . '

'Killin' ain't the first thing at all. Lookit what I got planned for Brett . . . But the day I can't outdraw Joe Vardis without missin' a chaw on my grub ain't dawned yet. Yeah — let's look into goin' through the high pass of the Diablos and down to Blanca. Sits better with me . . . '

The discussion didn't get much

further than that because one of the guards from the downslope came riding in fast, skidding his mount to a halt in a shower of stones and a cloud of dust.

'Boss! Boss — Two riders sniffin' around the water-hole between the ridges.' The man was gasping from his ride, swallowed, trying to get enough breath to add more and the three outlaws waited tensely. Finally, he blurted, 'One of 'em's Caleb Brett!'

* * *

The striking-looking blonde woman stepped out of the Las Cruces Mercantile, juggling a couple of parcels so that she could lift one hand to adjust her golden hair.

Actually it was an expensive French wig Coburn had brought back from New Orleans on one of his mysterious sorties that involved running slaves across the Gulf to Vera Cruz. He often sent or brought her presents when he had been away from her for a spell. She smiled secretly, thinking of the present she had waiting for *him* when she returned to the Springs after this chore.

She rather liked this job he had given her. Brought out the frustrated actress in her. Once she had thought she was going places on the stage but the only places she went were the beds of managers and writers and theatre owners — promising her a brilliant career, but all exhibiting mighty short memories after a few nights of ecstasy with her.

She finally admitted to herself that all she had were her looks, a body to drive even a preacher wild, an angelic face that never seemed to mirror the passing years and a certain talent that couldn't very well be displayed on stage — although she had had some offers at one time to go down to South America and do just that . . .

But Laurel Denise Westerman had drawn the line at that, despite the promise of big money. She had come to terms with herself and her lack of stage talent one day and decided she might as well exploit what attributes she did have as well as she could.

She used them to cheat a gambler out of some winnings, headed way out west in Texas, changed her name and opened her first gambling concession in a saloon. Unfortunately, this had been forced to close as had three or four others, until, finally, 'for the good of her health', she fled to the wild country where she had met the outlaw Heck Coburn. She hardly knew to this day just why she had fallen for Heck and she sure had little love for Jumping Man Springs, but he had set her up there, gave her money and protection and — well, she had simply fallen in love with him for no good reason she knew of. She was willing to do anything he asked, anyway. Even to come here to Las Cruces under her real name of 'Miss Laurel Westerman' and do what Heck Coburn wanted. Or what Bannerman wanted, really — he wasn't the kind anyone said 'no' to and Heck needed him for this big job coming up so she was happy to do her part. Not that this was really part of the job, but it would keep Coburn in Bannerman's good books so it was all linked up in some way, she supposed . . .

'Ma'am? . . . Miss Sherry West?'

She stopped dead as the voice called her from across the street and tensed when she saw the scruffy-looking man wearing a sheriff's star coming towards her, doffing his hat to reveal lank, colourless hair.

Somehow she found her most charming smile. 'Why, sheriff, you must have me mixed up with someone else — My name is Miss Laurel Westerman.'

Blackman, sweating and puffing some from hurrying — and badly needing a drink — mopped his face with a balled-up kerchief and smiled lightly.

'Ma'am, I know that's the name you been usin' since you come to town, but I have reason to believe that you also call yourself 'Sherry West' back in

Jumping Man Springs, Texas — and where you also seem to know an outlaw name of Heck Coburn.'

She was stunned by his words, her face unable to cope with the shock quickly enough to hide the fact. Folk passing by on the boardwalk drifted to a stop, to stare and watch and listen unashamedly.

'We can talk in my office, ma'am,' Blackman said leaning close and causing her to recoil from the sour blast of his breath. 'Fact is, there's a US marshal waitin' there who'd like a word with you, too.'

'This is ridiculous,' she said but she knew when to capitulate, too, and she could use the time it took to walk to the law office to get her story straight in her mind. No one had planned on this eventuality. She was just supposed to come here, do the job, and get out on the first available stage.

The US marshal's name was Needham and he had been sent to question Deputy Caleb Brett about the wrongful handing-over of Gil Bannerman to impostors claiming to be United States Marshals. Because they had been armed with the right papers and badges, they must have taken these items from the real lawmen, Foran and McMurphy, after murdering them.

Needham was not pleased that Brett had not waited for him to arrive but had taken off on a manhunt — mostly with the reward for Bannerman uppermost in mind, the marshal reckoned after speaking with Blackman and his daughter.

He had been as surprised as the sheriff when the telegraph message had come through from Van Horn . . . He glanced up now as Morg Blackman, shaking a little as his need for alcohol in his system became more urgent, came in with the blonde woman and introduced her.

'She denies bein' Sherry West, marshal, but she fits Caleb's description all right.'

Just then, Rose Blackman arrived

carrying a cloth-covered tray which she set on the desk. She glanced curiously at Sherry West and her father briefly explained.

'Oh — well, I've just brought dad and the marshal some lunch, Miss West. I can arrange some food for you if you wish.'

'No, thank you, I don't expect I'll be here long.' She turned to the sheriff. 'Did I hear you say Caleb Brett sent you a wire about me, sheriff?'

Rose, about to leave, stopped at mention of the deputy's name because the blonde woman had emphasized it slightly.

'Yep — from Van Horn, Texas. Said we was to keep you here till he got back. You're admittin' to bein' Sherry West now?'

She surprised them all by laughing throatily, smiling as she shook her head slowly. 'Oh, that Caleb! He's a sly one, isn't he?' At their blank looks, she let the smile fade slowly and added, 'Don't you see? He sent me here and this is

114

just his way of making sure I'll be here when he returns.'

'And just why would he want to do that?' It was Rose who asked, sounding very tense.

All eyes were on the blonde woman as she looked for somewhere to sit down. Rose's mouth tightened as her father stumbled in his hurry to drag out a chair for Sherry West. As she sat she set her parcels on the floor but gripped her fabric handbag tightly: Rose thought she wasn't as composed as she tried to appear.

'How well do you know Caleb?' Rose asked tautly.

'Oh, we've known each other for a couple of years now — You mean he's never spoken of me?'

'Not — one — word!'

The sheriff looked at his daughter sharply, spoke to Sherry West. 'Maybe you'd best explain, ma'am.'

'*That* would be nice!' gritted Marshal Needham.

The blonde woman was sober-faced

now though there seemed to be some kind of amusement lurking way back in her green eyes. 'I guess Caleb must be keeping it as a surprise . . . our wedding, I mean.'

'You lie!' Rose was shocked, white-faced, and her father hurried to put a comforting arm about her shoulders.

Sherry frowned. 'I'm sorry, Miss Blackman, if I shocked you, but I assure you it's true. Caleb and I are planning to be married this Christmas. Why, he's building a place for us just outside of this town . . . I hope to have a look at the land before I leave, as a matter of fact.'

Blackman and Rose seemed too stunned to speak. Needham noticed this but, not yet sure what was going on, held his peace. But it was difficult, for he was basically an impatient man.

'I know Caleb borrowed a good deal of money to buy the land and stock and the lumber for the cabin . . . I have — business interests in Jumping Man Springs, but Caleb, as you probably realize, is a proud and independent man and refuses to let me use any of my money ... ' She sobered now, a crease appearing between her eyes. Then she smiled, glancing up, spreading her hands. 'But it's all right now: he gave me the money and sent me up here to pay off his debts while he tried to pick up the trail of Bannerman and Heck Coburn.'

'Glad you mentioned Coburn,' the marshal cut in before either of the others could speak. 'I heard you were his woman.' He was a big man, towered menacingly now.

Sherry lowered her eyes, fingers plucking at her handbag. 'I — was. For a time. For longer than I desired, actually. But it's hard to break away from a man like Heck Coburn. I admitted everything to Caleb, of course, and he wasn't afraid to meet Heck face-to-face.'

'They've had a shoot-out?' asked

Blackman quickly, but the girl shook her head.

'No, no — ' She was visibly uneasy now. 'Look, I think I've said enough. I have nothing more to tell you.' She turned to Rose. 'I'm sorry if I upset you, Miss Blackman, but I had no idea you felt so — strongly about Caleb. I'm sure he doesn't either. I mean he's never mentioned . . . '

Rose's small hands bunched into fists down at her sides and tears welled up in her eyes. 'Caleb is going to marry *me*! He's building the ranch for *us*! I've never even heard of you!'

The sheriff just managed to hold Rose back as she made as if to lunge towards the blonde woman. Sherry West feigned surprise and even a little fear, pleased with her acting ability.

'I don't know what's going on.' She looked appealingly at the old sheriff and then turned her helpless gaze to the younger marshal, who looked to be a hard, tough forty-plus.

But if she expected sympathy or

understanding from Needham, she was sorely disappointed. 'How did Brett come up with that money to square his debts?'

Sherry looked haunted under the three hostile stares, shook her head with bewilderment. 'I — I don't know. It was a complete surprise to me.' She suddenly tilted her chin. 'But you may depend Caleb came by it honestly.'

'I ain't so sure,' Needham said curtly, eyes narrowing. 'And neither are you . . . It wouldn't be because it was given to him for makin' the 'mistake' of turnin' Bannerman over to them fake marshals, now would it? A pay-off — which would also explain why Brett didn't wait for me here — he wanted to get back down to Texas and pick up the money Bannerman had promised him!'

'That's a lie!' snapped Rose, barely able to hold back the tears now. 'Dad . . . ? You know that's not true!'

Blackman shuffled embarrassedly.

'Well — I dunno, Rose. It was kinda queer, Caleb handin' over Bannerman like that.'

'Dad!'

Needham moved in on Sherry West's chair, towered over the small and worried blonde woman. 'You know more than you're sayin'. I'm gonna hold you in the cells while I look into this.'

Sherry was aghast. 'Put me in jail? You can't do that!'

'Watch me,' Needham reached for her but she stumbled out of the chair, backing away from the stony-faced lawman.

'Wait!' Sherry was pale, giving the performance of her life now — though much of her fear and anxiety was genuine. 'Oh, I *knew* it was wrong for Caleb to take that money when Heck brought it to him . . . ' She dropped her handbag suddenly and covered her face with her hands. 'Oh, God, what've I done now!'

The lawmen exchanged glances while

Rose glared tearfully at the other woman.

Needham placed a hand on Sherry's shaking shoulders. He spoke gruffly.

'You'd better tell us the full story.'

6

Head-on

They had spent most of the afternoon searching for tracks around the deep waterhole in the valley between two harsh, knife-edged ridges.

There were plenty of tracks for them to study, five different trails of them, but unfortunately they were animal pads where the beasts of the Diablo Sierras had come to drink, night and morning.

Ben Tully thumbed his hat back off his face as the shadows of the ridges began to fill the valley, stood and leaned against his horse while he built a cigarette. Brett was down on one knee, examining ground at the edge of some brush, several yards back from the edge of the water.

'Too many animals, Caleb — must

be the best water for miles around. They been comin' down from the high country, even, I'd say. There's some mountain sheep and goat sign in places.'

Brett stood and arched his back to unkink cramped muscles from the long search. 'Well, looks to me like it'd be a good place for Bannerman to get deeper into these hills. So many animal tracks they must cover any made by horses each time they come to drink.'

Ben nodded as he cupped a match flame in his hands and lit his cigarette. 'Yeah — got the same feelin'. This is the way into the hills if you want to keep the trail to a hideout secret. Thing is, I can't find a single hoofprint under all them wild animal marks. Not even part of a horseshoe's curve. I'd expect to find the odd segment not completely covered.'

Brett frowned, nodding in agreement. 'Been bothering me, too. Was wondering if we're looking in the right place?'

'You ask me, this has to be it, Caleb.

We scouted all along the ridges on the far side there, comin' in from Van Horn, and the trails soon peter out, most turnin' back on themselves. Reckon a man lookin' around figures the place is too rugged, not worth investigatin'. Guess that's how they've kept it hid.'

'Yeah — and this is a real lush valley.' Brett looked around slowly at the slopes, surprisingly covered in thick, healthy brush and stands of small timber, all of which provided cover for wandering wildlife — both two-and four-legged. 'Yeah, this place is a surprise, all right. I'd never heard of any green valley in the Diablos before.'

'I've heard there was such a thing, but I've never been this deep in here before. Chased a bunch of Comanche down here once, but they stayed on the north-west face, gettin' in among the rocks, the way they like. Never had no reason to cross that first ridge — till today.'

'Well, what d'you think? Camp here tonight, back in that brush, see what comes down to drink at sundown and at sunrise — and maybe during the night.'

'Yeah. Be a good idea for one of us to stand guard, I reckon.' Tully moved his shoulders briefly. 'Got me a creepy feelin' about this place. And it's gettin' kinda chilly.'

Brett agreed but said they'd have to make it a cold camp. 'Just in case,' he added.

And that told Ben Tully that Brett wasn't about to give up. That he, too, had a strong hunch they were in the right place to pick up sign that would lead them to Bannerman and Heck Coburn . . .

But they didn't do it that night and ate cold jerky and the last of the cornpone they had bought in Van Horn. From now on it would be hardtack, except for a couple of cans of beans still deep in the grubsacks. They washed their meagre meal down with water from their canteens, rather than going down to the waterhole where animals were already starting to come and drink.

The wildlife continued to come far into the night. The birds had settled in the timber soon after sundown but there were stealthy paddings and occasional grunts and snufflings well after dark as fourlegged animals crept in for their nightly drink. Some would slink away silently to their lairs and not appear until sundown tomorrow, while others would sleep in hides nearby and drink again in the mists of predawn before going back up the ridge for their daily gathering of food. Some, of course, would ambush smaller prey while drinking.

They tossed a coin and Tully lost, drawing first stint of guard duty.

Brett settled down in his bedroll amongst the brush, the horses staked out some five yards away on a slope of scanty grass. The grass was better and more lush closer to the waterhole, but there was not enough cover to leave them to graze there.

Brett checked his guns, laid his carbine along his side as he stretched out, pulled his hat down over his eyes and went to sleep. He had acquired the habit long ago of being able to snatch a little shut-eye almost whenever he wanted, in the saddle or not, and he had full confidence in Ben Tully as a guard.

Tully held his fully loaded rifle across his chest for a spell, then set it down beside him where he sat on a rock amongst other rocks, utilizing the deepest shadow. He longed for a cigarette but, to take his mind off the craving for tobacco, he began to think about Nancy, now growing heavy with their first child.

He didn't care whether it was a boy or a girl, as long as it was born healthy and strong enough to cope with the kind of hard life it would encounter on the frontier. And, of course, he wanted Nancy to have as little trouble as possible: his mother had never had easy births with her five children, or so he had been told, for she had died while giving birth to him.

His mind wandered for a spell back to his childhood on the Ohio farm with his father and brothers and sisters, and not forgetting the old Cheyenne who came down out of the lush hills whenever they seemed to need him most.

He had taught Ben tracking and his father had taught him how to shoot. Both things had made him restless, filled him with wanderlust, but a strong sense of obligation had kept him home on the farm where he was needed. Then his father had taken a bad fall from a horse, landed across a tree stump, busted himself up inside something pitiful. He had never recovered, of course, and before he had died he had given Ben his blessing to follow the wild trails he so desired . . .

The rest of the family had done the same after the funeral and armed with his father's rifle — the very one he carried now — he had set out to make his fortune.

Well, he hadn't exactly done that but he considered himself rich. He had his own place to work — although most of it was owned by the Las Cruces First Mutual Bank — and he had a beautiful and loving wife and now his first child was due in a few months.

The ranch wouldn't pay its way this season, but by next season he could expect some sort of profit — even a little would be encouraging. He had good friends, Caleb Brett high on the list, and usually enough food in his belly.

Yeah, he was rich, all right. Not many men could say as much and . . .

He hadn't heard a thing, lost as he was in his dreaming. But suddenly a coarse hand clamped across his mouth, pinched his nostrils, and he was lifted bodily off his rock, then hurled back against it with stunning force. He fell to his knees and something smashed into his face. There was another blow across the back of his head and, as he fell into the pit of oblivion, he vaguely felt hard blows thudding into his lean body . . .

He was out cold before his bloody face ploughed into the rough ground.

Caleb Brett, feeling secure with someone like Ben Tully standing guard, shifted slightly in his bedroll. Perhaps the small sounds of smothered violence from amongst the rocks reached down through the layers of sleep to disturb him a little. Or perhaps he heard the muted snap of a half-green twig under a carelessly placed riding boot as a dark shape made its way down the slope and into his sleeping area.

But the first he really knew of an intruder was when a rough boot toe slammed into his ribs and sent him rolling out of the blankets. Instinctively, he snatched up the carbine and swung it around one-handed, blazing a single shot in the direction of the dark shape. Someone yelled and the shape was slammed sideways, stumbling as the man reached out for support. He missed a rock he was aiming for and spilled to the ground, writhing.

Brett worked the lever, rolling, but there was another man he hadn't seen and this attacker jumped down from atop a rock and landed on the deputy with both feet.

The breath smashed from him and bright stars burst and streaked behind his eyes. He choked and gagged, and the carbine was kicked from his loosening grip. A big hand fisted up his shirtfront, yanked him half erect, and then a gun barrel slammed across the side of his head and he was sure his skull had burst open an instant before everything went black.

* * *

At first he thought it was still dark when he came to. Not that it was any fun doing it.

His head felt like it had been cloven to his shoulders with a blunt tomahawk. Every bone in his body ached or throbbed. He could pick the places on his legs and torso where boots had landed, driven by hate, he figured, judging by the degree of pain he was enduring.

He couldn't see at all! That was what gave him the first inkling that while it might well still be night time, he was blindfolded. And he was certainly bound hand and foot. His mouth tasted vile and seemed to be filled with something particularly foul. He was gagged, likely with some filthy rag stuffed into his mouth.

So the only senses left to him were smell and hearing.

Brett had seen enough tough situations to know that survival likely lay in the use of whatever senses he could avail himself of. So he sniffed slowly, not loudly, picking up the smell of woodsmoke, cooked food, beyond the odour of horses. He couldn't smell man-sweat, but he could hear men somewhere in the vicinity.

Someone was moaning in deep, semi-conscious pain.

'He'll go plumb loco when we turn him loose, Gil.'

It sounded like a voice he had heard before. A few seconds' concentrated thought that briefly pushed back the throbbing agony in his head and he recollected where he had heard that voice previously.

Brazos Station. When he had handed over Bannerman to the fake marshals. Yeah — it was Heck Coburn, though he had called himself Marshal Foran at Brazos . . .

The voice that answered him now was unmistakably Gil Bannerman's.

'I *want* him to go plumb loco. I want the son of a bitch to go clear outta his head. And just when he thinks he's gettin' it all under control — well, wait'll he finds out what's waitin' for him in Las Cruces.'

Both men laughed briefly and Brett

felt the lance of sickness drive deep into his guts.

Las Cruces! What had this madman done? What the hell was he talking about . . . ? Brett had no doubt *who* Bannerman was talking about: it was him. He was the outlaw's prisoner and they were making him suffer — but while he was suffering here, something was also happening back in Las Cruces.

Rose! She was his first thought. *Oh, God, don't let them try to get at me through Rose!* It was a long, long time since he had acknowledged the possibility there might be a God, but the prayer sprung instantly into his mind. *Don't let them harm Rose . . . Please!*

Hell's teeth, what about Ben Tully? The thought hit him like a kick in the teeth. He had been so busy with his own hurts and trying to figure out what was happening that he had momentarily forgotten Ben . . .

What had they done to him? Where was he . . . ?

134

The hurt man he had heard when he had first come round moaned again and that lance of sickness stabbed into him once more. *Ben* . . . ?

He struggled against his bonds and he heard boots crunch on gravel. Suddenly he was lifted a foot along the ground by a savage kick in the side. He grunted in pain, toppling from his sitting position.

'Now!' a man gritted not far from him and there was a choked, rasping sound and a kind of flapping that went on for a few minutes, and Brett lay there, trying to figure out what it was.

'Done, Gil,' a harsh voice said, a mite breathlessly.

Then Brett was kicked again, hauled half upright by his shirtfront and fists hammered into his face, a knee rammed his chest. He almost choked and rough hands pulled the gag free enough for him to breathe. Then the beating started again and jarring blows gradually hammered him back into the pit of blackness where he had dwelt these past hours . . .

He was still lying on his side when he came round, coughing spitting, the taste of sour vomit in the back of his throat.

'I think he's joinin' us again, Gil.'

Heck Coburn, his battered brain registered . . .

'How you like bein' a prisoner, Brett?' asked Bannerman, sounding pleased with himself about something. He punctuated the question with another kick in the side. 'Well, I operate different to you — I'm gonna turn you loose pretty damn soon. There'll be a couple of surprises for you . . . '

'Where's Ben?' gasped Brett, fighting the loosened gag.

'That goddamn tracker you brought along? Oh, he's hangin' around. You'll find him when you work the gag off again. Now we gotta be goin'. Got us a job to do. I'll be seein' you again, Brett. Lookin' forward to it.'

Brett felt himself frowning. 'What the hell is this, Bannerman? Why don't you finish me off right now?'

Bannerman laughed. 'You hear that, Heck . . . ?'

'He has a point,' Coburn said slowly.

Bannerman's voice had a hard, brittle edge to it when he spoke again. 'I *told* you what I had in mind.' Then Brett smelt the man's tobacco-breath as he leaned down close and spoke slowly. 'I ain't about to kill you yet, Brett. I owe you — and I always pay my debts. Just you wait'll you get back to Las Cruces, if you don't believe me. Or mebbe you'll believe me long before then! Adios, you bastard!'

The farewell kick almost drove Brett's ribs clear through to his spine. Then the gag was pushed back into his mouth . . .

When he came to the second time, he found the bonds had been loosened some, and the blindfold knot had also been shifted enough to allow the cloth to partly slip down his swollen nose. He tried working it down further by muscle contractions but he couldn't manage: it hurt too much.

Breath hissed through swollen, blood-clogged nostrils. One eye hurt sharply, puffed half-shut. His teeth ached and he tasted stale blood when he swallowed, stomach heaving. The gag was still in place.

Well, obviously he was meant to work himself free, so that was what he had better do . . .

It took him over half an hour and he had to have frequent rests, his head buzzing, vision blurred over one corner of the blindfold that he had managed somehow to work down just a fraction. He still couldn't twist around far enough to see behind him so he concentrated on manipulating his hands, working up a sweat to make the flesh slippery, using the lubrication to help slide the ropes down. It was a slow painful process and he took off some hide while struggling, but finally the ropes loosened, slipped over his fingers and dropped away one by one.

He tried to take his weight on his hands but they were too numbed and his wrists simply folded up and spilled him sideways. He endured the needle-sharp pain of returning circulation, blood-streaked face pressed against the hard ground. He then drew up his legs, knees to chest, fumbling at the ankle bonds with fingers that still didn't work properly.

He didn't know how long it took him but he paused once to yank down the blindfold all the way, saw a rough camp, a fire burned-down but still with embers. He hitched around on his rump after removing the gag. His throat was dry but he tried to call Ben Tully's name.

No answer. All he could hear, apart from insects in the nearby brush and a few distant bird calls, was a monotonous creaking, familiar but just beyond reach of comprehension.

It puzzled him until he got to his knees and straightened, blinking against the rising sun, glimpsing movement. *Ben*, likely gagged the way he was, which would be why he hadn't answered. He squinted hard against the harsh light.

'I'll have you free in a minute, amigo,' Brett rasped, starting to crawl towards the vague movement, the creaking seeming to grow a little louder as the morning breeze touched him and made him shiver involuntarily.

Then he realized the blurred movement seemed to come from slightly above him. He'd thought it was because he was on hands and knees, but it was higher than that.

Squinting, grunting with pain when he tilted his head, he froze when he saw a pair of dirty, holed socks and frayed trouser cuffs moving back and forth in front of his eyes in a short, rhythmic arc.

'Oh, my God!' he breathed, almost afraid to look up.

Belly knotting, he sat back on his hams and slowly lifted his gaze up Ben

Tully's legs, past the torn and bloody clothing to the swollen, empurpled, battered face with the staring eyes. Just showing above the tilted head, was the top of the knot in the rope that had been thrown over a tree branch before they'd hung the young tracker.

He'd been tortured and beaten first.

★ ★ ★

It was a hell of a ride back to Las Cruces.

The outlaws had left him his guns and mounts when they had abandoned him but no grub or water. He had collapsed while trying to cut down Ben Tully, didn't know how long he was out to it, but the sun seemed pretty damn high when he finally came round. There was a mouthful of water in one canteen and he used half to swill out the foul taste and swallowed the rest.

While he had been unconscious, the rope knot had slipped and Ben had fallen in a heap, the ants already crawling on his clothing and into the cuts and gashes and bruises from the beating he had taken before the hanging.

Caleb Brett brushed the young tracker down as well as he could, wrapped him in a blanket and strapped it up tightly, dragging the body away from the ants' nest. It almost exhausted him and he realized just how much of a beating he had taken himself at the hands of Bannerman.

The man was plumb loco, sadistic. Why had he killed Ben and not him . . . ?

That was when he remembered Bannerman promising him a 'surprise', waiting for him back in Las Cruces . . .

The knowledge galvanized him into action. Ignoring his hurts as much as he could, he struggled and fought for most of the day to get Ben draped over his mount and tied in position. He gathered his gear, took time to search for tracks, although the strain on his good eye made it water and burn.

He figured there had been five of them camped here. It was obvious this was a temporary camp, likely well away from any permanent one they might use in the Diablo Sierras. Five men — and what had Bannerman said? Something about they had to go because they had a job to do . . . What kind of job? he wondered. But he was too exhausted to hold the thought, moved like a man in a daze, mounting old Zack — only after several tries he had finally had to stand on a rock so as to clamber into the saddle.

It was dark when he started down the slope, letting the bay have its head, figuring the horse's instincts would lead it to water.

It did so, coming out at the same waterhole in the rugged valley where they had been jumped by Bannerman's crew.

He drank and filled his canteens, fashioned a snare across a small-game trail and retreated into the timber. He passed a restless night and when he woke he was almost too stiff to move, muscles cracking and aching. The cold had bitten deep into his bones but there was a racoon caught in the snare and he skinned and gutted it and cooked it over a small fire, spitted on a stick.

He was ravenous and ate it all. The horses had found grass for themselves and luckily they gave him no trouble, coming to his calls.

Then the long trail back to Las Cruces began.

He stopped briefly at Van Horn, traded Ben Tully's old rifle for grub and coffee and a check-over by a doctor. He thought about sending a wire on to Las Cruces, but some instinct warned him not to let anyone know he was on his way back.

Brett didn't know why he felt there might be danger, but something nagged at him and he left Van Horn in the afternoon, taking as direct a trail as possible back to the state line.

He was two days on the trail and Ben's body wasn't a pleasant companion, although he unloaded it twice and let it soak in a stream during the night in an attempt to slow down corruption.

He was gaunt and weary and still somewhat stiff from his battering when he finally sighted Las Cruces late in the afternoon, sundown hazing the air above the town, giving it a faint peach-lavender glow that made it far more attractive than it actually was.

Brett debated about camping out tonight and going in early the next morning, but decided against it. He wanted to make sure that Rose was all right, even if it meant he was walking into danger.

So he rode on down and the streets were shadowed and painted with the deep amber-gold of after-glow when he put the bay up to the hitchrail outside the law office.

Men were already gathering, word having spread that Brett was back with a body tied over a horse. Most folk hoped it would be Gil Bannerman's corpse, but Brett refused to answer the questions thrown at him by the gathering townspeople.

The commotion brought out Sheriff Morg Blackman and Brett felt the relief flood from him so that his legs turned to water when he saw Rose beside him.

She started across the walk towards the deputy but then the big frame of Marshal Needham appeared, pulling her back as he confronted Caleb Brett.

'That ain't Bannerman,' the marshal said, indicating the blanket-wrapped body.

'No — wish it was. It's young Ben Tully.'

There was a murmur ran through the crowd and Rose grasped her father's arm tightly. But the marshal suddenly drew his six-gun and covered the startled Brett.

'I kinda figured it might be — least-ways, I was pretty damn sure it weren't gonna be Bannerman . . . '

'What's the gun for?' Brett asked warily.

Needham moved fast, took a step forward and whipped Brett's Peacemaker from his holster.

'Caleb Brett, I'm arrestin' you for aidin' and abettin' the escape of a wanted outlaw — and for acceptin' a bribe to do so . . . Now don't gimme no trouble, feller. Just lift them hands and march on into the law office. We gotta cell all ready and waitin' for you.'

7

The Nitro Express

They had not only set him up but had wrapped him up tight as an Egyptian mummy, Bannerman finishing things off with a neat little bow.

In the delicious shape of Sherry West.

She should have been on the stage, the way she acted when Blackman and the marshal, with Rose hovering in the background, brought the blonde woman into the passage outside Brett's cell.

He had been stretched out on the bunk, still stiff and sore from his beating and the long ride in. He half-raised his head off the thin straw pillow when he heard someone coming but sat bolt upright despite his hurts when Sherry West suddenly lunged for the cell door and gripped the bars. He was quite startled when she began crying.

'Oh, Caleb, I'm so sorry! I — I didn't mean to let it slip about Heck giving you the money but — I did and then he . . . ' She paused long enough to stab a gloved finger in Needham's direction, using her other hand to dab at her eyes and moist nostrils with a wisp of lace. 'He forced it out of me! . . . I — I didn't mean to make trouble for you! Can you ever forgive me?'

The trio in the passageway behind the blonde woman stared at him, Blackman with a frown, Needham's expression cold and hard, Rose bewildered but with a flickering flame far back in her eyes.

Brett walked stiffly across the cell and while he spoke to the marshal, his words were really directed at Rose.

'What's going on? I've never seen this woman before in my life.'

Sherry gasped, looked horrified, and then gave a tremulous smile. 'Oh, I see what you're trying to do,

Caleb — But, it's too late, darling. Too late — Because of my foolishness!' There was a fresh outburst of sobbing and her shoulders shook, real tears sliding down her contorted face.

Brett, shaken and trying not to show just how much, looked directly at Rose now. 'Rose — I swear to you, I don't know this woman! I guess she's Sherry West, because a man in Jumping Man Springs told me Heck Coburn had sent her here, but . . . '

Sherry West lowered her kerchief, blinking at Brett. 'Caleb, what're you saying? *You* sent me here. With money Heck Coburn paid you for turning over Gil Bannerman to him and Gabe Blanchard! I knew it was wrong to take it but you said it was all arranged and that I should ride here to Las Cruces and pay off your debts so we could get married earlier than we'd planned . . . '

Brett actually reeled, put a hand to his throbbing head, shaking it slowly. 'Judas priest, I dunno what's going on!' He looked appealingly at Needham. 'Will you listen to what really happened?'

'I'm willin' to let you have your say,' the marshal said while Sherry West's mouth tightened and she tilted her jaw at Brett and said, 'Yes — I think I'd better hear it, too.' She flicked her gaze towards the silent Rose. 'There's something going on here that I don't like!'

'You're gonna like this even less,' Brett assured her and began telling his story, ending with Ben's hanging. He had been watching the blonde woman's face and it bothered him some to see the emotions flitting across those quite lovely features: horror, disbelief, a twinge of jealousy when his betrothal to Rose was mentioned . . . *She should've been an actress*, he thought after he had finished, waiting for Needham's reaction.

'Why did you go after Bannerman?' the marshal asked, taking him a little by surprise.

'Why — to bring him back, of course. I'd made the mistake of handing him over to Coburn. I figured it was up to me to bring him back.'

'Yeah, it was,' Needham allowed but before he could say more, Sherry West broke in, her voice shaking.

'I don't like this, Caleb! This — this is not what I expected! I warned you it was foolish to go after Bannerman when Heck Coburn had already paid you money. I told you the reward didn't really matter . . . I have money but you're — you're so damn proud that . . . '

'Rose, it's all lies!' broke in Brett desperately. 'Can't you see Bannerman did this? It's his way of getting back at me because I captured him and . . . '

'He had you a prisoner. He hung Ben accordin' to you,' said Needham coldly. 'If he wanted to get back at you why didn't he string you up, too? Or put a bullet in you?'

Brett sighed. 'He's loco. It's not the way he thinks. He wants to destroy my life slowly, frame me with this — woman and money I've never seen.'

The people in the passageway went silent and Rose stifled a sob. Brett was aware of a coldness spreading through his belly.

'What's wrong . . . ?'

It was Rose who spoke. 'Caleb — Marshal Needham found two thousand dollars hidden in the bottom of your saddlebags.'

Brett's mind reeled. 'I never . . . ' He stopped, seeing it was no good, shifted his gaze quickly to Sherry's face and surprised a calculating triumph in her eyes which she quickly covered by dabbing with her lace kerchief. His shoulders slumped. 'That son of a bitch really nailed the coffin lid down tight, didn't he? That money was planted on me.'

'Is that all you have to say?' Rose asked, lower lip all a-tremble.

Brett stared steadily at her. 'There don't seem much else I can say right now, Rose — You believe her, not me.'

'What am I supposed to do?' she cried, a sob almost choking her. 'She knows all about you. Says you've known her for two years . . . I see now why you went to Texas so often!'

'Well, I'm not a bigamist, Rose — Why would I get betrothed to two women at once?'

'Oh, I don't know!' she broke into uncontrollable sobbing and flung herself down the passageway. Her father went after her, pausing only to throw a savage look at Brett.

'By God you'll pay for doin' this to her! I'll make damn sure of it!' Then he hurried after his daughter, calling her name.

Brett bit off the curse that rose to his lips and glared at the blonde woman. 'If I ever get my hands on you, I'll choke the truth out of you!'

Then *she* burst out sobbing, too, covered her face and hurried out of the passageway.

Needham looked mildly amused but underneath he was cold and hard.

'Worst thing I know is a corrupt lawman, Brett. If this turns out to be all true, I'll see you hang for the murder of Ben Tully.'

'For Chrissakes, I didn't kill him! Bannerman did!'

'I reckon I can make you an accessory if nothin' else.' He lifted a hand quickly as Brett started to protest. 'Maybe Tully couldn't be bought so he was strung up . . . You're lower'n a snake's belly far as I'm concerned, Brett.'

'Look, why the hell would I ride in here with such a story if I'd sent the West woman on ahead to square my debts . . . ?'

'Hell, you weren't expectin' her to've slipped up and told the truth about that money. *And* there's the little matter of the two thousand in the bottom of your saddlebag . . . You want to explain that?'

Brett gritted his teeth. 'I can't, except I know it was planted on me.'

'Sure, by Bannerman — He'd spend

all that money just to mess up your life?'

'I tell you he's loco! It's the kind of crazy thing he would do — just to get back at me. Killing me would be too quick as far as he's concerned . . . '

'Aw, shut up, Brett! Just — *shut up*! You make me sick to my stomach! You're gonna stay locked up till I get the straight of this — one way or another.'

As the marshal started down the passage, Brett gripped the bars and called, 'Two thousand's nothing to Bannerman! I recollect now being half-awake and I heard him and Coburn talking. They're pulling off some big job that's gonna set 'em up for life!'

'You just happened to remember this, huh?' Needham said, shaking his head and brushing Brett's words aside with a cutting motion of his hand as he went on down the passage and through to the front law office.

Slowly, Brett returned to his bunk and sat down on the edge, rubbing his

fingers against his throbbing temples.
'God-*damn*!' he said feelingly.

★ ★ ★

The man sitting behind the bush halfway up the steep slope of the mountain trashed his cigarette butt and snatched up the battered leather-and-brass field glasses from the ground beside him. It was drizzling rain and he swore when he found the lenses were fogged. He wiped them on the inside of his shirt, wishing he'd brought a slicker with him for this lookout chore.

He focused on the distant movement out on the prairie and his lips peeled back from stained and chipped teeth.

'By God, Heck was right — they put out the schedule for tomorrow, but sent the train a day early to foil any hold-up attempts!' He laughed. 'An' a lot of damn good it did 'em!'

The man's name was Beech and he forgot all about his discomfort — he had been sitting in the inadequate shelter of the bush for four hours — and slung the binoculars around his neck by the leather strap, picked up his rifle and started down the slope. It was slick with the rain, which had started after he had gotten into position, and he slipped and slid most of the way down on his backside.

He was muddy and breathless when he stumbled into the outlaws' camp under the cottonwoods, seeing that they had rigged a square of tarp to give some protection from the rain.

'She's comin', Heck!' Beech yelled as he slid and scrambled up the slight rise to the camp. 'Way out right now, but headin' on in sure as it's rainin'!'

There were five men, including Bannerman and Coburn and Gabe Blanchard, who didn't look any too happy about being here. His concussion was still troubling him and he complained his vision blurred frequently or went double, and he felt nauseous. None of which got him any sympathy from any of the others.

The only reason Blanchard had made the effort to ride on the job was because he knew Bannerman had meant it when he said he didn't get a share unless he did.

The men were moving about now, breaking camp, talking amongst themselves, grinning with excitement and nervousness as the time approached for the robbery.

Bannerman went to a square leather box with a series of straps and buckles on it that was sitting on a piece of flat ground, held at the base by flat-sized rocks. He lifted it carefully, took it to his horse and strapped it on the saddle so that it hung where normally a saddlebag would be, but, because of the extra straps, was held much more firmly.

It amused him to see how the others gave him a wide berth as he settled in leather. He laughed.

'Save your energy, fellers! Gettin' a few feet away won't save you if this stuff goes up. It'll flatten every tree for a hundred yards and there won't be enough left of you to make a flea sneeze.'

Still they hung back and let him lead the way, the rain coming down more heavily now, rattling loudly against their stiff slickers.

Heck Coburn made sure his slicker covered his guns.

Although he had worked with Bannerman on several other occasions, he still didn't trust the man. He was a little left of normal at times although he gave the impression of intelligence. Heck knew it was more an animal cunning that had gotten the man his reputation, that and a willingness to kill ruthlessly, leaving no witnesses — or to kill for any reason if it came to that. Or no reason at all.

He just wasn't sure that Bannerman was going to stick to the deal. The temptation for a bigger bite at the apple, maybe all of it, was there. He wondered how many of the others were thinking along the same lines . . .

Beech — dumb but a killer, only OK if he knew *exactly* what to do. Big Red Halloran with the outsize belly and food-clogged beard and the ugly face: all he could think about was women and the only way he could get *any* women interested in him was to dazzle her with money, a lot of money. Whitey — young, fast with a gun, kept to himself so a man couldn't be sure just what he was thinking — but he sure liked to spend up big when they hit a town to paint it red . . .

Gabe Blanchard — well, Gabe was Gabe. Hard at times, but essentially a ninny when it came to any kind of hurt. He'd likely quit after this job, Coburn figured.

And Heck Coburn? The outlaw smiled to himself as they walked their mounts down into the narrow cutting. Well, Heck Coburn wasn't a greedy man, but if he saw a chance to get himself more than one share of this loot . . . well, he sure aimed to grab it quick as a cat catching a blue-tailed fly . . .

Bannerman had already dismounted behind the rain-darkened sandstone boulders when Coburn walked his horse in and swung down from the saddle, keeping the shotgun barrels tilted down so no rain would get in. He carefully held the gun under the folds of the slicker as he watched dry-mouthed while Bannerman casually unstrapped the leather box and let it swing from its harness.

He saw Beech's eyes bulge a little and Whitey ran a tongue around suddenly dry lips. Gabe still sat his horse: he never did dismount or mount any more than was necessary.

'Hey, easy with that stuff, Gil!' Big Red said, sounding hoarse. 'No sense in takin' risks, man!'

'Relax — I got it all nestlin' in cotton. I could drop this and it wouldn't go off — Leastways, don't think so!' He laughed shortly.

'I'll take your word for it,' Whitey allowed, voice cracking a little.

Bannerman shook his head slowly. 'Hell, this ain't the most dangerous stage. Biggest risk is when you're boilin' the dynamite and scooping the nitro off the top. It's why they sometimes call it soup — not that I'd care for a bowlful of this stuff, mind!' His blood must be *singing* with excitement . . .

'Just quit all this playin' around,' Heck Coburn said, irritated — *and* scared, he admitted but only to himself. 'The train'll be in the cuttin' before we know where we are. Now get into position . . . And, Gil, don't use that stuff 'less you have to.'

Bannerman arched his heavy eyebrows. 'I'll *have* to. There ain't no other way. It's why we tried it three months back.'

Coburn frowned but nodded. 'Yeah — I guess. But make sure the rest of us are outta the way before you set it off.'

'If you're where you should be, there won't be no danger,' Bannerman said indifferently and, whistling, started towards the low part of the cutting, beginning to climb the slippery slope.

Big Red swore.

'That crazy bastard's gonna get us all killed if he don't stop clownin' around!'

'You know what he's like with nitro,' Heck Coburn said heavily. 'Makes him more loco than he already is. Now do what we have to, but stay well back from that special car . . . You never know just when Gil's gonna decide to toss that nitro around. Look what happened last time . . . Bodies everywhere.'

They spread out to pre-planned positions and even above the clatter of rain on their slickers now they could hear the distant throb of the locomotive as it made the wide curving swing in towards the cutting.

They hunkered down, ignoring the rain where it found rents in their slickers and trickled coldly down their unwashed bodies, hands numb where they gripped the actions of their weapons, listening to the train coming closer — closer . . .

The note changed when it entered the cutting, the echoes of the clattering wheels and the panting of the loco taking on a drumming sound.

The waiting men tensed, all eyes on the bend halfway through the cutting, already seeing the black streamers of smoke curling up into the leaden skies.

Then the loco appeared, the cow-catcher first with its specially-built flat iron platform for the armed guards and lookouts to stand on. There were four men, soldiers wearing yellow, glittering slickers, their guns under the oilcloth to protect them from the weather.

Coburn snapped his head around to the left, to the slope above the track where the timber was heaviest. What the hell was wrong with Red and Beech . . . ? By now they . . . *Ah*!

Suddenly one of the biggest of the lodgepole pine trees quivered, then teetered, and Coburn, because he was looking for it, saw the rope spray a long line of silver rain squeezed from it by the tension, and then the partly cut-through tree fell with a crash right in front of the locomotive.

It was too late for the engineer to do anything but react instinctively and slam on the brakes. The rails being wet the iron wheels failed to grip and the hundreds of tons of iron and timber and coal that went to make up the train slid forward at barely diminished speed, ploughing into the fallen tree, branches snapping and splintering — and wiping the four armed guards off the front of the train. Three were caught, two being impaled by splintered limbs, the third being crushed against the hot boiler of the loco. The fourth man managed to leap wildly aside and he landed just down the slope from where Heck Coburn waited. The man, white with shock, mud mixing with blood from a cut on his face, staggered upright, awkwardly throwing back his slicker flaps, bringing his gun around. Coburn gave him both barrels of the Greener and the man was blasted back half beneath the still sliding locked wheels of the train. The forward motion sliced him in two.

Then the loco hit the heavy trunk of the tree and while it partially pushed it aside, it did not clear the line properly and the train shuddered to a halt, panting hollowly, the front wheel bogey jumping the rails.

The bruised trainmen saw the outlaws coming out of the rocks and brush and the engineer tried to ram the lever into reverse but Big Red Halloran leapt onto the footplate, dropped him with two bullets to the back of the head. The brakeman dived out the opposite door but Beech was waiting and although the shocked man staggered upright with hands raised shoulder-high, the outlaw cut him down coldly.

Coburn ran along the line of tarp-covered freight cars to the special grey-painted sheet-iron carriage that had a single word painted on the big sliding door: *Express*.

There were bars over the small windows and already gun barrels were poking through those bars as the armed men inside sought the outlaws who were trying to break in.

'You want to live you'll push your guns out and open that slidin' door!' Coburn said, crouching close against the car, looking for sign of Bannerman on the cutting wall, not trusting the man.

If he tossed down his nitro bottles now, it would not only blow open this iron-shod car, but conveniently kill Coburn and the others as well.

'Go to hell!' a man yelled from inside, triggering his rifle several times uselessly.

'We'll blast our way in and that means you'll die — No job's worth that!' Coburn called again.

'You won't blast your way in here!' the same voice answered and then a gun on the other side roared and a man cried out.

'Who was that?' Coburn demanded.

'Whitey,' called Beech. 'Sonsabitches got him when he tried to run up the slope!'

Coburn swore. 'Stay where you're s'posed to be and no one'll get hurt — 'cept those fools inside! You hear me in there?'

'Same answer, you coyote! Go — to — hell!'

'You'll be there first!'

Coburn was moving even as he spoke, lunging for the nearby rocks, zigzagging as rifles spat death at him from the iron car. The bullets zipped into the ground around his pounding feet and he hurled himself headlong, sliding in the mud. He was about to call out to Bannerman to drop the nitro when he swore and squirmed deeper into the rocks.

He glimpsed two falling black shapes against the rain clouds as they dropped towards the roof of the iron-clad express van and its only two weak spots — the skylights which were partly open to allow air to be scooped into the van.

'Get down!' roared Coburn but the

words were drowned in two thunderous detonations so close together they smashed through the narrow cutting in a single deafening roar.

When the smoke cleared, the long express van had been torn open as if by a giant can-opener, the roof gone, the side walls bulging and sagging with jagged, torn sheets of iron dangling dangerously. The big sliding door lay halfway up the slope, buckled and smeared with gore that was all that was left of Big Red Halloran.

Now they only had to split the loot four ways, providing Beech and Gabe Blanchard were still alive.

Otherwise, it would be just between Bannerman and Coburn.

And Heck didn't much care for his chances of staying alive long enough to enjoy his share if that was the case.

8

Out!

Caleb Brett strode from one end of his cell to the other. Damn it to hell! he thought. He couldn't tolerate this much longer.

It wasn't just the confinement, it was the *reason* for it. Framed neatly by that goddamn Bannerman and Heck Coburn. Not forgetting Sherry West. By God, she was quite an actress. She had convinced Needham and Blackman without half trying. Rose wasn't far behind, either . . .

He stopped pacing, grimacing slightly as he recalled the visit by Rose to his cell. She had waited until nightfall, came while her father was supposed to be on duty in the front office. Well, he was there — but occasionally Brett could hear the clink of bottle neck against glass and he knew that Morg was hitting the booze again.

'I saw Nancy Tully on your behalf, Caleb,' Rose started quietly and he figured briefly that she was having second thoughts about this crazy deal. 'She's most upset, of course, collapsed at the news. Her mother's staying with her but I waited for a while and did what I could to comfort her. She says she doesn't blame you in any way — Ben wanted to go, was glad of the chance to secure their future by earning the reward money for Bannerman — but it's a terrible blow. She has no money, you know. Ben owed the bank and the Stock Association . . . '

'Get me out of here, Rose!' Brett said, gripping the bars so tightly his knuckles were pure white. 'If I'm out I can track down Bannerman and Nancy can have the reward. I know it's little enough to do and it can't replace Ben but I feel responsible no matter how charitable she says she feels about it.'

Rose's face tightened. 'You ought to know better than to ask me such a thing, Caleb! Specially after how you've deceived me all this time.'

It was like a mule-kick to the belly: hell, she hadn't changed her mind at all. It was just her innate decency that brought her here and that had sent her to see Nancy on his behalf. But, damnit, *she still believed that West woman*!

'Rose, for God's sake, you *can't* believe Sherry West! I swear to you I'd never laid eyes on her before I saw her in the front office.'

'Oh, Caleb, why keep up this pretence? You were always down in Texas, *looked* for excuses to go . . . '

He nodded, sighing. 'That's true — Rose, Morg ain't the easiest man to work for and he gets maudlin and whining when he hits the bottle as you know — I was just looking for excuses to get out in the field for a spell, that's all. I wasn't doing it so I could go visit Sherry West. Hell, I've heard about her

173

gambling place in the Springs and the women she keeps in the upstairs rooms but . . . '

'Running down her character won't change things, Caleb,' Rose said sharply. 'She knew too much about you. The ranch, the money you owed the bank and so on . . . You must've confided in her. How else could she know those things?'

He shook his head, made a helpless gesture. 'Bannerman could've picked it up while he was here in jail. Like I said, Morg is a whiner and he whined a'plenty about what a hard life he has to lead, all within earshot of Bannerman . . . '

She had stiffened, her mouth drawn into a thin line. 'I think it's despicable to speak about Dad that way! He's getting old and he's — sick and . . . '

'He's a drunk, Rose. Face it. He's a drunk and he's manipulating you and me so's he'll have someone to take care of him . . . '

'Well, that's a daughter's duty — *You*

certainly aren't being asked to do *anything*!'

Then she had turned and flounced out, leaving him staring through the bars with mouth agape . . .

Now, in the dimness of the cell on the second night, he cursed softly. He hadn't seen her since and Blackman had refused to give her any messages and Needham was only interested in getting solid proof of the charges of graft and corruption against him.

And all this time, Bannerman was on the loose and laughing, living it up no doubt with Heck Coburn's bunch . . .

There was movement at the end of the passage and he glimpsed a silhouette against the patch of light from the glow of the lamp in the front office. He saw a swirl of skirts and heard a woman's footsteps hurrying along towards his cell door.

'Rose!' he called, vast relief in his voice as he went to the barred door.

But his face stiffened when he saw it wasn't Rose at all. It was Sherry West.

'What d'you want?' he growled. 'I got nothing to say to you.'

She smiled as she stood outside the door. 'Not even 'thank you'?' she asked mockingly and he blinked as she produced the keys to the cell door, holding them and jangling them together.

Brett stiffened, gripped the bars with both hands.

'What's this?'

The girl looked exasperated. 'Come on Brett, don't act the fool. You can see what I've got here.'

'Like to know where and how you got 'em.'

She smiled and spoke soberly. 'I got them off the wall peg behind the sheriff's desk in the front office . . . I'd heard he liked a drink so I simply supplied him with a couple of bottles and now he's happily snoring in his deskchair.'

'Why?'

'Damn, but you can be an irritating man, Brett!' She leaned forward slightly

176

from the waist, jangling the keys again. 'I'm going to set you free.'

He was immediately suspicious. 'Why would you do that after going to all the trouble of getting me put in here?'

The mocking smile faded. 'Maybe I found a teensy-weensy bit of conscience I didn't know I had . . . '

'I dunno as I'd swallow that.'

'Then why the hell worry about it? You want to stay put, let them keep you here while Needham's out having all the fun?'

He frowned. 'What's that mean?'

'I guess nobody told you — Gil Bannerman and Heck Coburn held up the Fort La Union pay-train out in Coffee Can Cutting . . . Killing everybody on board except the train guard and left a few of their own men dead, too. Someone used nitro — Guess that'd have to be Bannerman. He always did like playing around with explosives.'

Brett was silent, assimilating the news.

'Marshal Needham's taken a posse and gone out there looking for tracks. The word is he's going to try to tie you in with it somehow . . . I didn't mind setting you up for a bit of trouble with your girl and so on, but this — well, it goes against my grain.'

Brett didn't believe that, thinking she was capable of just about anything, but he wasn't going to be loco enough to say so right out loud at this time. Maybe *after* she opened the cell door . . .

'Well, I appreciate the sentiments, Sherry, I surely do — You gonna open the door for me now?'

She shook her head, surprising him. She laughed at the stunned expression on his face.

'Oh, relax, you'll be out in a few minutes — But you'll have to do it yourself. I want to be quite a distance from this town by the time you step out of that cell, Caleb Brett . . .

'You don't trust me?'

She snorted. 'You nor any other man.'

'Except Heck Coburn.'

'Not even him — Not with all that payroll money involved. I aim to be on hand when they divvy up. I don't intend to stay around here playing Miss Prissy while they ride off with the loot . . . '

Jaw hard, Brett looked at her steadily in the dim light. 'How you going to do it?'

'Mmmmm — Think I'll go back to the bend in the passage and then toss the keys back towards your cell.'

'They might land short, where I won't be able to reach them.'

She looked past him into the cell. 'Use your head — You've blankets on the bunk. Try tossing one end over the keyring and dragging it towards the cell door.'

'The flagstones are uneven. They could catch up . . . '

'Oh, for God's sake, Brett! I don't have time to stand arguing with you. Just figure it out for yourself. This is the only chance you're going to get.'

179

She turned and hurried back to the bend in the passage. He saw her silhouette as she paused, tossed the keys towards his cell. They landed with a dull clank some six or seven feet away from the cell door.

'Not close enough, damnit!' he called.

She moved away without speaking but was back in a minute and he heard a clatter as she threw something else down the passage.

The office mop. It landed just past the keys. He might be able to toss a blanket over the mophead and, holding the opposite corner, drag it to within reach. Once he had the mop he could use it to pull the keys towards the cell door . . . Good thinking on Sherry's part.

He hoped.

He glanced up, but the girl had already gone.

It took him almost half an hour to get the keys.

He couldn't believe such a simple

retrieval would take so long but the mophead was wet and so heavy it tended to cling to the surface of the flagstones as well. Consequently, the threadbare jail blanket kept trying to simply slide off rather than grip it and pull it towards him.

He tried straining through the bars as far as he could reach, tried to toss the end of the blanket over the keys but they were too far away. Next he began tossing the blanket over the long mop handle and while he was successful in dragging it closer, once it turned at right angles to the cell, the blanket fabric could no longer grip it.

He was sweating and breathing heavily and his arm ached. He was also starting to panic a little, hearing Blackman's snoring take on a grunting, coughing sound. Something fell with a clatter. Hell! Was the sheriff waking up . . . ?

He knotted the other blanket to the one he held and while he could reach the mophead and the keys, the end just slid off as before. In desperation, he tied a bulky knot in the end he had been throwing at the mop and keys and this time it caught on the wet strands of the mophead and actually moved it a foot or so before it slid off. Three more tries and he caught it again, dragged it around and gave a sudden yank, jumping it over the irregularities in the flagged floor. It landed three feet outside the barred door and two more throws and he had it in his grasp.

A few minutes later he had pulled the keys to within reach and he opened the cell door, snatched his hat from the bunk and moved quickly down the passage.

Looking into the law office, he saw that the street door was closed and, best of all, Morg Blackman was fast asleep in a drunken stupor, tilted way back in his chair.

Moving swiftly, confidently and quietly, Brett took his guns from the locked cabinet, swallowed a mouthful of whiskey that remained in Blackman's bottle and grabbed his saddlebags and bedroll from a corner.

He went back down the passage past the cells to the rear door, dropped the bar, used the keys to unlock the door and slipped out into the night.

They had stabled the bay in the old sheds behind the jail and his saddle was hanging on a stall partition. Six-gun in one hand, reins in the other, he led the saddled gelding out of the stables and across the weed-grown back yard to the sagging fence. There was no rear gate in the fence, the stables being reached down a side alley from Main Street, but Brett didn't aim to go out that way, even though the town seemed quiet.

He found the sagging panel in the fence that he wanted, worked on it until the rusted nails pulled free and then eased the heavy oblong of palings to the ground.

Leading Zack over this, he made his way afoot to the corrals behind the livery stables. He ground-hitched the bay and went into the livery by the back door. All was quiet, a couple of lanterns burning in the aisle, another in the office cubicle to his left. He could see the legs of the night man in there, figured it would be the kid, the livery man's son, a vague boy in his late teens but who still liked to play with girls' doll's houses. A gentle, smiling man-child.

The boy was asleep, his too-short bib-and-brace overalls soiled, one bony leg dangling over the edge of the narrow bunk. Brett shook it until the boy opened his eyes and blinked, staring a few moments before smiling in recognition.

'Deputy!' He rubbed his eyes. 'I been asleep. You won't tell pa, will you?' He sounded anxious about this last.

'No, Lonnie, I won't tell — Say, did you rent a hoss to a nice-looking blonde lady tonight? She was wearing a dark green dress and a little hat that kind of cocked over her left eye.'

Lonnie frowned, then shook his head.

'Nope, never did hire a hoss to no lady in a green dress, deputy . . . Should I have . . . ?'

'No, it's all right, Lonnie, just an idea I had.' Brett sounded disappointed. 'You go back to sleep — and don't tell anyone I was here, all right.'

'I won't — if you don't tell pa I was asleep.'

Brett grinned, placed a hand on the boy's thin shoulder and squeezed. 'Deal, Lonnie. You go back to sleep now.'

He turned and was just leaving the office when Lonnie said, 'She was wearin' a dark blue dress and a grey hat with a wide brim, tied under her chin with a fancy silk ribbon. Weren't no green dress, deputy.'

Brett turned sharply, smiled slowly. 'She must've changed, Lonnie. Last time I saw her she was dressed in green. When did she pick up the horse . . . ?'

It took time but near as Brett could figure, Sherry West had taken the horse almost an hour ago and she had ridden south out of town . . .

'That hoss shoulda been shoed,' Lonnie volunteered. 'Left foreshoe is wore down at the front. Pa ought've shoed that hoss yest'y but he was too drunk . . . '

Brett smiled his thanks: now he knew what kind of tracks to look for . . . He hurried out into the night.

★ ★ ★

Brett knew he couldn't trail Sherry West at night so he concentrated on getting out of town without being seen. He was pretty sure he made it, but he rode in a south-west direction just in case anyone did spot him — or came looking for his tracks come daylight.

Lonnie wouldn't give him away. The kid was scared white of his father and wouldn't risk the man finding out he had been sleeping on the job. He was a strange kid, none too bright in some ways, but there was a lot more to him than appeared on the surface and Brett had always gotten along well with Lonnie. They had made a 'deal' and he knew the boy would stick to his end of it.

So when Morg Blackman came round and found out he was gone from his cell — and that likely wouldn't be until morning — Brett planned on being a long ways from Las Cruces. In any case, Blackman wouldn't ride with any posse: he would be too hungover for one thing, but hadn't been riding out of town for any reason for a long time now. The word on the streets of Las Cruces was that he didn't want to get too far from a bar . . .

So Caleb Brett camped cold in an arroyo in the foothills, crossed the range this side of sunup and angled down to the trail that led due south while there was still only dim grey light. By the time he found the first sign of Sherry West, it was bright and promised to be a hot, cloudless day.

The blonde woman had ridden this

way, all right, heading straight for the state line, wanting to get back to Texas in a hurry. She might be making for the Springs, but Brett had a notion she had some other place in mind first.

She seemed to know all about the outlaws' plans to rob the pay-train, so presumably she knew their escape route and he figured she might be going to meet up with them. Which would suit him just fine . . .

She was riding fast and the worn shoe was showing signs of stress. He figured it was coming loose as the nail-head impression was getting deeper. If it threw the shoe she would be stranded somewhere ahead.

Just how far ahead would depend on how long she had kept riding last night. She may have ridden through the night and be holed up during the day, hoping to throw any pursuit. Then again she might just be riding as fast as far as she could before the horse needed a rest.

The tracks told him she had pushed the horse hard and there were definite signs that that front shoe was going to give her a deal of trouble before she got too far down into Texas.

He found sign that told him the nail had come out and he back-tracked some and found it, bent out of shape, a few feet to one side of the trail where it had been thrown. That shoe wouldn't last another mile, he figured, but he only travelled half that distance before the shot crashed from the rocks a little way up a ridge and he heard the bullet whip by with a faint snarl.

It was a six-gun, about a .36 or .38 calibre he judged by the crack it made when the second shot whined off a rock beside the bay, making it leap sideways with a sharp whinny. He plunged the mount into the boulder field, dismounted behind some brush, sliding his carbine out of the saddle scabbard.

A third shot ricocheted wastefully from the boulders, but he made his way around the far side, crouching, running quietly, sliding down a small slope into a dry wash.

At the end of this, he bellied up into the clump of rocks where he figured the shooting was coming from and moments later he saw her.

She was dressed as Lonnie had described, blue dress and grey hat, holding a Smith and Wesson pistol awkwardly as she strained her upper body to see over the rocks, searching for him.

He snapped the carbine's hammer back, deliberately letting her hear the click as it cocked. She spun wildly slipping, the pistol thundering into the air. Before she could get up, his right boot was pinning the Smith and Wesson to the ground and the carbine barrel pointed between her breasts. He shook his head slowly.

Her eyes blazed up at him. 'I knew it would have to be you! If that damn horse hadn't thrown a shoe . . . '

'Too bad.' He scooped up the pistol and rammed it into his belt. 'Well, not too much of a problem to figure out where you were headed — Going to Jumping Man, weren't you?'

She remained silent although he asked the question several times. Then he shrugged. 'Hell, I don't have time to pussyfoot around with you, Sherry. I've got things to do.'

'Where're you going?' she cried in alarm as he walked away. 'You can't leave me here!'

'You watch,' he answered without either turning or pausing.

She was on her feet now, ignoring the dust and grit clinging to her skirts. 'Wait up, Brett! Please!'

He turned impatiently.

'I — I know where they're going.'

'Bannerman and Coburn?' At her nod, he waited expectantly.

She smiled with a little edge of triumph. 'I'll show you, but I'm not fool enough to simply tell you.'

After a pause he nodded. 'All right — I can fix your horse's shoe temporarily. We can cut across to Brazos Station and likely find a new shoe in the old smithy . . . ' Suddenly he grinned. 'That's it, ain't it? They're stopping off at Brazos Station.'

She tossed her head. 'Nothing of the sort . . . But, yes, I think we should shoe my horse there if it's possible.'

Brett smiled, made her stay within sight while he straightened the horse-shoe nail and hammered it back into the worn shoe.

They rode slowly, side by side, the girl obviously thinking of running but having enough sense to know her horse could never outrun old Zack with its worn shoe.

They came in sight of Brazos Station in late afternoon and when they were just short of a half-mile from it, the girl suddenly spurred her mount forward, lashing it with her rein ends, shouting, 'Shoot him, Heck! It's Brett! Shoot him!'

Nothing happened but she kept riding fast for the yard and tumbledown buildings of the old waystation.

Then suddenly a rifle crashed in a single shot.

And Sherry West was blown clear out of the saddle, tumbling and skidding for several yards before she flopped in an untidy heap, skirts and petticoats all awry.

9

Another Way

Brett quit leather in a plunging run, snatching his carbine as he went. He stumbled, almost fell but recovered and dived headlong behind some low rocks beside the trail.

One more shot thundered and the bullet whined away, throwing powdered rockdust across his hat and shoulders.

Rolling, he flopped onto his belly, carbine coming down between two rocks, elbow digging in as he levered a shell into the breech. Gunsmoke rose from behind the ruins of the well and he sent a shot towards the place, just to let the man know he had him spotted: there was no hope that he could hit the ambusher from the angle he was firing at right now. By the time he had jacked another shell home the rifle out there hammered twice more and, moving fast, Brett had rolled to the very end of the pile of rocks. From here he could see partly around the end of the well wall — and behind it was a rusted, though heavy-gauge iron earth bucket that had likely been used to dig the well in the first place and for clearing obstructions and foul matter at a later date.

It looked solid enough to Brett and he took careful aim below the first line of rivet-heads. Before he could squeeze the trigger, the killer fired but his aim was off and hard on the sound of the shot, Brett's carbine whiplashed, once, twice, three times as he levered and triggered swiftly.

He saw all three bullets leave silver streaks on the rusted bucket, red dust flying where they impacted, and then they ricocheted — at least two of them towards the well. There was a startled cry, a grunt that choked down into a moan of pain. Then he saw the rifle spill out from behind the well wall, followed by a man's hand and part of a grimy shirt sleeve. The hand lay on its back on the ground and the fingers twitched only once or twice and then were still. Brett kept his sights on the bucket a spell, then placed a careful shot right beside that motionless hand. It kicked briefly into the air and flopped back.

Satisfied, he stood, carbine at the ready, and whistled Zack to him. He walked beside the horse towards where the body of Sherry West lay in the dust. Her mount stood quivering some ten yards away, ears erect, eyes wide and wary. It snorted and shook its head and the bay answered. Then Brett was kneeling beside the girl. He carefully turned her over onto her back. She cried out in quick agony and he grimaced when he saw the blood on her blouse front. The shot had taken her through the lower left breast and was pulsing bright and fast. He tore off his neckerchief and wadded it over the wound. She was alive but unconscious, her face scarred by the gravel she had fallen on.

He lifted her in his arms and walked in towards the station buildings, the bay and Sherry's horse following slowly. Brett's gaze scanned the station buildings and he jumped when a gust of hot breeze slapped a door on one of the old storesheds. But there was no sign of a second bushwhacker and he set down the girl in the shade of the porch, using her hat for a pillow, and turned back to the well.

A man lay there, his back torn open by ricocheting lead. There were two big wounds, one in his side, the other in his back, and when Brett turned him over he saw there was another, older wound in his head. A bullet crease that he had bound up with strips of filthy rag. He recognized him as a man he had seen on a Wanted dodger at ranger headquarters in Wagonmound. He thought he was called Beech or Beecher. In any case, he was dead now, so names hardly mattered.

Brett prowled the outbuildings and found two jaded horses, one with dried blood on the saddle, in the old barn. Immediately alert, he made for the main building, the only place he hadn't searched. He went in carefully, using the gun's barrel to push open any doors. There were bloody rags on the floor in the kitchen, signs of a fire in the rusted cooking range, the ashes barely warm. He made for the bedrooms down the passage.

The door creaked as he prodded open the first one with the carbine's barrel and he jumped back, heart ramming up into his throat as a six-gun filled the room with brief thunder. The bullet tore a long dagger-like splinter from the door and Brett crouched, carbine ready to fire. But there was only the one shot and it was followed by a sick moan and then the thud of a heavy object falling to the floor.

Craning his neck some, he saw a smoking Colt lying on the floor beside a bedframe with a straw-stuffed mattress on the rawhide straps that acted as springing. There was a man lying on the bed and Brett stood slowly as he recognized Gabe Blanchard.

There was no one else in the room and Gabe had bloody rags tied about his chest and one arm and one side of his face was torn and bloody. He looked like a dead man waiting for the final call to Glory.

'You're a mess, Gabe.'

The outlaw rolled his head towards the sound of Brett's voice. 'Who's that? I — I can't see. Got hit on the head with somethin' blew off the train durin' the explosion an' I'm blind.'

There was fear in his weak, hoarse voice. Brett still covered him with the carbine. 'You got caught in the nitro blast, is that what you're saying?'

'It's Brett, ain't it? Yeah — recognize your voice, damn you! Well, I — I guess you're better'n — Bannerman.'

'He leave you for dead, Gabe?'

'Yeah, the sonuver — Ol' Beech he wanted to bring me along. But

Bannerman said no and Heck went along with him. When Beech argued, Gil shot him . . . but the bullet only creased him. Then they blew the safe and rode out with the dinero.'

'Where were they headed, Gabe?'

'Here — Brazos Station. Aw, they was bound for Sierra Blanca, gonna lay low with Joe Vardis — but they don' trust a snake like Vardis so decided to stash the — loot — here . . . ' He paused, fighting for breath, making wheezing, gasping sounds.

'Beech got me on a hoss an' patched hisself up and we come here. He said their tracks showed they was only hours ahead of us . . . Then he went lookin' for the cache and I heard the shootin' . . . '

'And almost blew my head off when I came in the door . . . Did Beech find the money?'

Gabe went quiet, except for his rattly breathing. Brett prodded him with the gun barrel and he moaned.

'Aw, hell, don' do that! — I'm all

busted up. I'm — dyin'.'

'Yeah, Gabe, you are — So that money ain't gonna do you no good. Tell me where it is and you'll have the last laugh on Bannerman.'

'Why should I make it — easy for you, Brett?'

Brett shrugged, forgetting the man couldn't see. 'Why worry about that? It was Bannerman and Coburn who did this to you. You can make sure they don't get the money from that train before you cash in your chips — Might make your going a mite easier knowing that.'

'What — what're you gonna do with it?'

'I'm still a lawman, Gabe.'

He was surprised when Gabe actually tried to laugh but he choked in pain and it seemed a long time before he spoke again, his voice weaker now.

'Way I heard it, you're an outlaw — That was part of Bannerman's plan for Sherry to bust you out, get you on the run, make you look guilty . . . '

Brett's mouth tightened. 'Yeah, well they did that, all right — but if I recover the stolen payroll I'll be all right.'

'Like I say, why should I — hel — help you?'

Brett sighed. 'Up to you, Gabe — But I can take time to look around. Oughtn't be too hard to find some place that's been disturbed recently . . . I'll eventually find the cache.'

'Then — you do — that,' Blanchard gasped.

Brett nodded. 'Nothing I can do for you, Gabe. So long.'

Brett went out, back to the porch where he had left the girl. He drew water from the well and washed her wound, ripping up her skirts to make bandages and wads. She was yellowing and breathing raggedly, shallowly.

He went back to the well and dropped the wooden pail in, needing a drink badly. The rim caught on something but before he could free it he heard horses coming and snatched up the carbine, crouching near Beech's body behind the rock wall.

A bunch of riders were homing in on the station, coming fast, though their mounts showed weariness, being pushed to the limit. It didn't take long for Brett to recognize Marshal Needham and the sixman posse was made up of men from Las Cruces. They reined up fast when he stood and let them see the carbine.

'Needham — it's safe to come in. But forget any notion of taking me prisoner — There's a heap of explaining to do.'

'Damn right!' Needham snapped. 'And you can start by tellin' me what in hell you're doin' here instead of back in the Las Cruces jail where I left you!'

They came in slowly, weary, red-eyed, dusty, the townsmen nodding to Brett. Needham looked grimfaced, badly wanting to reach for his six-gun but still covered by Brett's carbine.

The deputy explained quickly, standing close to the wounded woman.

Needham's face didn't change, except his eyes slitted down some.

'You expect me to swallow that hogwash? Seems to me you had a rendezvous planned here with Bannerman but he crossed you — and Blanchard and Beech, too.'

'Damn you, Needham, show some sense! I . . . '

'He's — speaking the — truth — Marshal.'

All eyes turned to Sherry West. She looked ghastly, lying in the shade, fighting for every breath. Two men went inside to see if there was anything that could be done for Gabe Blanchard.

'It was all — all lies — Bannerman wanted — revenge on Brett — I set him up — Then turned him loose — Gil knew — he would be branded — outlaw — Got some kind of — weird kick out of that — Knew Brett would — come after him . . . and he wanted that, too. Wants to ruin Brett's life first, though . . . Gloat before he — kills him . . . '

She fell silent, fighting for breath, clinging tightly to Brett's hand when he knelt beside her, wiped her face with a wet cloth.

'S-sorry,' she whispered, closing her eyes.

'It's all right,' Brett told her, glancing up at Needham. 'I don't think he believes you but thanks for trying, Sherry. I'm obliged.'

One of the men who had gone in to see to Blanchard appeared in the doorway. 'Gabe's gone,' he announced and Needham swung his gaze back to Brett.

'And he died before he could tell you where Bannerman and Coburn had stashed the money, huh?'

'Goddamn, but you're a suspicious son of a bitch, Needham!' Brett snapped wearily. 'No, he never told me where the money was hid but I think I know . . .'

'You think.'

Brett swallowed a curse and turned back to the well. He leaned over and jiggled the rope. The bucket rim was still caught on something. He looked over his shoulder as the marshal came up behind him.

'Down there?' He sounded more reasonable of a sudden.

'Could be. I think it's on a ledge just under the surface. Foran's body was caught up on it when that mountain man found him . . . '

'Someone better climb down and check it.' Needham stared hard at Brett who sighed. 'You're younger'n me, deputy.'

'OK — Here. Hold my carbine.'

'Might as well take your Peacemaker, too.'

Their gazes locked then Brett slowly unbuckled the heavy gun rig and handed it to the marshal. He swung his legs over the side of the well and slid down the wet and slimy bucket rope. He lowered his legs into the water and when he felt its coldness reach his waist, he leaned down, plunging his face under, groping in the shadows.

There seemed to be a natural rock ledge. His fingers touched the edge of an iron-bound chest.

Gasping, he rose out of the water and called up, his voice booming back to him. 'It's there. But we'll have to be careful. If it slips off it'll go straight to the bottom.'

'It — better — not,' Needham called back. 'You get a rope around the handle and do it good, Brett — You might say your entire future depends on this.'

Well, that was something, anyway, Brett allowed silently.

It was the first time that Needham had hinted he might be willing to believe Brett's story if he recovered the stolen payroll . . . Then a rope end came coiling down to him slowly.

* * *

'Jesus Christ, they've found the strongbox!'

Heck Coburn felt as if his head was

about to explode as he adjusted focus on the battered field glasses, lying prone on top of a sandhill as he watched the activity about the well down there in Brazos Station's front yard. 'Brett's down in there with a rope, goddamnit!'

Gil Bannerman was stretched out a few feet away, watching through his own glasses. He said nothing, just continued to watch the posse's efforts to recover the box.

'Damnit, I told you it was too obvious a place to stash it!' griped Coburn.

Still Bannerman said nothing.

Coburn stretched his lips across his teeth and muttered curses to himself. They had been well on their way to Sierra Blanca, after stashing the strongbox at Brazos. He had no gripe with that: taking that much money, almost a hundred thousand, within ten miles of someone like Joe Vardis was just the same as committing suicide. In fact, suicide would be a damn sight less painful than Vardis's method of torture.

But while that ledge just under the surface of the well water was convenient, Heck Coburn had been against hiding the strongbox there. Everyone who came to the old way-station took water from the well and while it was unlikely that the level would drop, there was always the chance the bucket would catch on the edge of the box where it overhung the ledge.

Looked to him like it had happened that way. It was the shooting that had brought them back across the dunes to the station. It was slow travelling through that hot, loose sand with near-jaded horses, but they had to see what was happening.

Both had been surprised to recognize Beech sprawled out dead behind the well's wall and Sherry West lying on the porch. Coburn had almost started to go down there when Brett had appeared and tended to the woman. Bannerman had laid a hand on his arm and pointed to the dust cloud approaching from the north-east. It could only be a posse, but they hesitated to run for it.

Finding out if the money was still safe was uppermost in their minds . . .

Now it seemed it had been discovered. Coburn's fingers almost cracked with the effort he put into holding the field glasses as Brett climbed up out of the well, dripping. Then a couple of men winched up the rope and the strongbox appeared, trailing silvery ribbons of water . . .

'Christ, that's it! All for nothin', Gil!'

Bannerman, still watching, said quietly, 'We ain't lost it yet.'

'What're you talkin' about? We got no hope of takin' it back from that posse! That's Needham, down there, one of the toughest marshals ever rode this neck of the woods.'

'I know Needham,' Bannerman growled. 'Owe that bastard plenty, too — You give up too damn easy, Heck.'

Bannerman rolled onto his side and Coburn frowned as he saw the man was focusing his glasses now on something to the north. He glimpsed a yellow dust-devil and frowning, raised his own glasses to see what was making it.

'There's your answer, Heck,' Bannerman said with a cold kind of excitement. 'Couldn't be better!'

Coburn sucked in a breath as he brought the two riders into focus. They were out of sight of the waystation but the outlaws could see them clearly now as they rode through an arroyo, a ridge between them and the station.

It was Sheriff Morg Blackman — and Rose.

10

A Kind of Justice

Rose was very tired but immensely proud of her father. She looked at him now as they rode between the eroded walls of the long, twisting arroyo which would eventually lead them to the ridge which stood between them and the old Brazos Station.

When she had discovered that Brett had escaped — or been turned loose by that West woman, it later seemed — she had run back to the front office to shake Morg Blackman out of his drunken sleep.

He had blinked and stared vacantly as she spoke urgently.

'Dad! Dad, you have to wake up properly! Caleb's gone! D'you understand me — he's not in his cell . . . He's — escaped!'

It took some time for it to filter through the sleep-and-alcohol befuddled brain and she searched around desperately, found a bottle with a mouthful of whiskey left in it, slopped it into a dirty shot-glass and forced it into his hands. He looked at her gratefully with a crooked smile, used both hands to get the steadying drink to his slack mouth. Spilling most of it, he still got enough down to shudder and to bring him back to reality.

His voice sounded like a hacksaw cutting into metal when he spoke. 'Es-caped . . . you say?'

She took him by the hand, dragged him into the dim cell block. He stumbled over the breakfast tray she had brought for Brett and Blackman stared at the empty cell.

'I — I never let him out,' he slurred, bewildered.

By that time, Rose had coffee poured and handed him a cup, urging him to drink. She explained that this was how she had found the cell when she had arrived, Blackman still asleep in the office chair, no signs of violence.

'You'll have to get a posse together and send them after Caleb, Dad.' She knew well that he hadn't left town on any riding duty for months. 'He — he might be with that woman . . . '

Her father said nothing, gulped the coffee, saw the anguish on her face, the tears filling her eyes. Suddenly he shook himself. It didn't make him feel any better but maybe the knifing pain from his aching brain would keep him alert.

'No, Rose. It's my fault he escaped — I was drunk when I should've been watchin' the jail . . . It's my job to bring him back.'

'Dad!' She was shaken, startled. 'But you — you haven't ridden for months!'

'Then mebbe it's time I did it again before I forget how.' He forced a smile and put a shaky arm about her shoulders. 'I know how worried you are about Caleb, daughter . . . I still dunno the straight of that thing with the West woman. I seem to be thinkin' a mite clearer this mornin' than usual, somehow. I reckon we gotta give Caleb a chance to explain — No, no, don't say nothin'. But you know we ain't given him much of chance to really explain his side of things . . . Guess we can blame Needham for that, but we gotta shoulder some of it ourselves . . . '

She smiled as tears tracked down her smooth-skinned face. 'Oh, Dad! I — I'm so proud of you! And I'm coming with you!'

Well, that started an argument but here she was, riding at his side in her split buckskin riding skirt, cream blouse and buckskin vest, her face shaded by her narrow-brimmed hat. Her father looked the worse for wear but he was determined and it was this resolve that encouraged her.

It might be just what he needed to get him back onto the straight and narrow again, put some pride back in him, make him feel like a real lawman again . . .

He had taken a guess that the trail would lead to Brazos Station after finding the tracks and reading them surprisingly well, including the stop where Brett had re-shoed the West woman's horse. He also said the sign indicated that the West woman wasn't coming willingly, that she had made several attempts to veer off.

'Looks to me like they been arguin',' he told Rose. 'And could be that they weren't really in anythin' together — I mean, she left town long before him . . .'

Rose knew he was only trying to cheer her up and she smiled fondly at him. But she *wanted* to believe he was right . . . desperately so.

Then they reined down suddenly, both seeing at the same time the two armed men who walked their horses out from behind a rock outcrop, setting their mounts squarely across the trail.

'By Godfrey!' Morg Blackman hissed.

'That's Bannerman! And Heck Coburn!
. . . *Ride*, Rose! Get outta here!'

He leaned out of the saddle, slapping
his hat across the rump of Rose's
mount as he snatched at his six-gun
with his other hand.

Her horse skittered away, startled,
and she was so unprepared that she
actually hauled back on the reins. So
she saw the whole thing.

How her father came upright in his
saddle again, jumping his mount away
from hers so that the outlaws' guns
followed him, his Colt coming around
clumsily across his body as he fired.
They must have let him get off that one
shot for both men grinned before their
rifles crashed. Coburn's fired only once
but Bannerman levered and triggered
several times, putting bullet after bullet
into the tumbling body of Blackman as
he spilled from the saddle.

He was dead long before he hit the
ground and Rose's scream echoed back
down the arroyo as Coburn spurred
forward, leaned from the saddle and

grabbed her mount's bridle.

'Now where you think you're goin', lady . . . ?'

* * *

The gunfire in the arroyo hadn't carried over the ridge to Brazos Station and the posse were still gathered around the iron-bound chest. It had been moved to the porch.

Needham had detailed two men to rig a travois to take the wounded Sherry West to Fort La Union for medical care.

Brett didn't think she would make it. She had lapsed into unconsciousness and was sweating, her face doughy and drawn with much pain. Although the wound wasn't bleeding much, outwardly, the way she coughed wetly and rackingly every so often made him think there was still internal haemorrhage.

Needham wasn't really interested in her welfare. He seemed willing to accept her brief statement that she had set up Brett on the orders of Coburn and Bannerman, but he still had a hostility about him, especially towards Brett.

The man was obsessed with nailing Bannerman, Brett figured, and would go to any lengths to get the outlaw.

Now he looked up at Brett. 'You know, Bannerman's gonna have to come back here.'

'Sure,' the deputy said slowly. 'If he wants to collect the loot.'

'So?'

Brett signed for the marshal to go ahead and Needham's eyes narrowed.

'So why do we have to go traipsin' all over the country after him? We just sit and wait.'

'Now hold up, marshal!' said one of the posse men instantly. 'I've come a lot further than I reckoned on already and been away longer'n I wanted to be — My wife's due a baby any day and . . . '

'Then go back,' Needham told him

curtly. 'Go back and you don't share in the reward.'

The man looked down at the ground. 'We-ell, I'd sure like a share of that bounty, marshal, but my wife's had a bad time of it already and — well, I shouldn'ta come in the first place. I keep worryin' about her all the time.'

Needham ignored him and turned to the other three townsmen. 'Anyone else want to go with him now's the time . . . 'Cause we'll be diggin' in here for a spell.'

One of the three, a youngish man with a cleft chin, asked, 'How much longer, marshal?'

'For as long as it takes Bannerman to come back and pick up his cache.' Needham sounded mighty belligerent.

'Yeah, but — a coupla days? A week?'

'Could be longer,' Brett said, earning himself a savage look from Needham. 'Gabe said Bannerman and Coburn were gonna lay low with Joe Vardis down in Sierra Blanca. So that could mean anything — a couple weeks, mebbe a month.'

'As — long — as — it takes,' gritted the marshal.

The three men grumbled and the marshal continued to glare at Brett. The deputy met and held his gaze.

'Waiting for a month would be plumb loco, marshal — We could take a big posse down to Blanca and drag Bannerman back in much less time. Be a better move I reckon.'

'You think a lizard moves out here without Joe Vardis or Bannerman knowin' about it? Hell, a posse that big wouldn't get across the state line before Bannerman'd break for the border.' He scowled. 'Anyway, he wouldn't wait that long. He's too money hungry. He'll be wantin' to spend it. Likely he'll try to kill Vardis, maybe Coburn, too. But he'll be back in a week or so. We can hole up yonder in the rocks and nail him when he rides in.'

'Count me out, marshal,' said the man with the cleft chin, suddenly. 'I

221

reckon it'll be longer'n a week. And I can't stay out another week, anyways. I'll lose my job.'

'The reward'll keep grub on your table.'

'*If* we get Bannerman. S'pose he brings Vardis with him?'

The other two seemed uncertain now. They each wanted to share in the bounty, but Needham had driven them savagely and there was no reason to suppose he would be any easier on them just waiting for the outlaws to return. Anyway, Bannerman *might* come back with Vardis's bunch and they would be outnumbered and . . .

The upshot was that all townsmen voted to return to Las Cruces and their families. Needham told them to get then, and to stay out of his sight. He glared angrily as they gathered their gear and rode after the men taking Sherry West to Fort La Union. Then he rounded on the deputy.

'Thanks a helluva lot, Brett!'

Brett shrugged. 'They'd run if

Bannerman came riding in alone, you know that, Needham.'

'Aaaah . . . All right, let's get this strongbox back in the well so's we can jump 'em easy while they're tryin' to get it up again.'

Brett held up a hand. 'Wait a minute.'

The marshal, starting for the still-wet box, frowned at the deputy. 'Well?' he snapped impatiently.

★ ★ ★

They had only just finished putting the box back in position when Brett caught movement out of the corner of his eyes. He glanced over his shoulder casually, mopping sweat from his face, and stiffened.

A rider was bringing his horse down the steep face of the nearest red sand dune. There was a white rag of some kind tied to the barrel of his rifle.

'Judas! That's Heck Coburn!'

Needham, dusting off his hands,

223

spun quickly, reaching for his six-gun swearing briefly. 'Now what's that sneaky son of a bitch up to . . . ?'

'That's meant to be a flag of truce,' Brett pointed out as the marshal cocked his pistol.

'You think Coburn'd recognize it if it was you or me ridin' in with a rag tied to our rifle barrel?'

'I dunno — But *I* recognize it. He wants to powwow.'

Marshal Needham's mouth pulled into a razor slash as he watched the outlaw coming in slowly, warily. They could see now that he had the lever action open on his rifle, indicating it was empty. There was no six-gun visible although he wore bullet belt and empty holster.

'Likely in his saddlebag where he can get to it,' opined Needham. 'Or stuck in his belt at his back.'

'We better hear what he's got to say.'

'Listen, Brett, you're a pain in the butt to me. I'm the senior man here.

You defer to me . . . And you follow my lead.'

'Not if it might blow the whole deal.'

Needham looked as if he would swing his Peacemaker onto Brett but he held back with an effort, turned towards Coburn. '*We* make the deals, not him.' He raised his voice.

'What do you want, Coburn?'

'I'll come in a little closer.'

'You'll do what I tell you! And I'm tellin' you to stop where you are!'

'Damnit, Needham, bringing him in closer would be the wiser thing.'

'You're the one worried about the flag of truce, and now you want him where you can jump him easier!'

Brett sighed exasperatedly. 'Only if it's some kind of trap. But we need to find out. With luck he won't know the others've gone. He might think they're somewhere inside.'

Needham had made the men leave the spare horses and they were now in the tumbledown corrals. But Coburn slowed and waved the rifle so they would be sure to notice the white flag. Brett frowned. It looked like a woman's scarf . . . His stomach lurched. Not white, but cream. And silk. Just like one he'd bought for Rose in El Paso one time, to go with a riding blouse of the same colour . . .

'What is it, Heck?' he called hoarsely and the sudden tension in his voice brought the marshal's head snapping around.

'We want the strongbox. We seen you get it outta the well . . . And we seen you puttin' it back. Where you send Sherry, by the way? La Union, mebbe . . . ?'

'Something like that,' Brett answered. 'She's pretty bad, Heck — Where'd you get that scarf?'

Needham frowned, swallowing the words he was about to say. Heck Coburn, beard-shagged, face dirty from long, hard riding, grinned, his teeth showing white against the grime.

'Think you recognize it, do you,

Brett? Well — could be you're right. See, Gil and me figured we'd do a straight swap. One for one.'

He hitched in the saddle, lifted the rifle high above his head and waved it in a slow are from side to side, twice.

He was staring up at the crest of the big red dune rising behind him.

The lawmen switched their gazes to the crest, too, and a moment later two figures appeared, a man and a woman, the woman's arm being held by the man who had a gun in his hand and as they watched he pressed the muzzle against her head.

'Hell almighty!' breathed Brett. 'That's Rose!' Needham nodded silently, jaw thrust out, eyes pinched down. Brett snapped around to look at the smirking Coburn. 'How the hell did you two get your hands on her . . . ?'

'Guess she was comin' after you — Had her old man with her. We jumped 'em back in that arroyo beyond the ridge.'

Brett was very still now. 'Morg was with her . . . ?'

'Yeah — Old fool tried to play the hero. You believe it? The town drunk tryin' to protect his daughter and dyin' doin' it.'

'By God, you just admitted killin' a lawman, you murderin' son of a bitch!' growled Needham, starting to bring up his gun.

Brett moved in fast, knocked his arm down but the marshal's eyes blazed and he swung angrily. The gun clipped Brett across the side of the head, knocking off his hat. Dazed, he fell to his knees and Needham stepped away from him, snapping the gun down to line up with Coburn who was about to spurt away.

'Hold it! I've got you cold, damnit!'

'You blamed fool! Look up on the dune! Bannerman'll blow that gal's head off without missin' a drag on his cigarette if you try anythin' with me!'

'Won't matter much to you, Coburn, by then . . . Just like the gal don't matter much to me, not as long as I can nail you two!'

Coburn swore, wheeled his mount, snapping his rifle lever closed and Brett, staring through a red haze of pain, wondered if there was a bullet in the magazine after all, just waiting for the closing of the lever to jack it into the breech . . .

He hurled himself at Needham, knocking the man sprawling as he fired. His shot was wild and Coburn raced for the dune. Brett pushed to his knees, looking for Bannerman but both he and the girl had dropped from sight. Coburn hipped in the saddle as he set his mount climbing through the steep, loose sand.

'You got one hour! Get up that strongbox or the gal dies! We ain't bluffin', Brett!'

Needham snapped another shot at Coburn and the outlaw fired his rifle, just the one shot, then concentrated on riding up the face of the dune.

Marshal Needham swung his smoking

pistol at Brett's head again and the deputy ducked under his arm, hammered two slashing blows to the man's midriff. Needham grunted, staggered, almost fell. Brett twisted the six-gun out of his grip, flung it aside as the marshal lunged up and swung a kick. The boot caught Brett in the shoulder, spinning him off-balance. Needham plunged after him, fists hammering.

Brett dropped suddenly, kicked the man's legs out from under him. As Needham stumbled to hands and knees, Brett drove a punch into his ribs, knocking him onto his side. He rammed a knee into the man's chest, smashed aching knuckles against the lantern jaw. Then he grabbed the long hair and pounded the man's skull into the hard ground several times until he saw the eyes roll up whitely into their sockets.

Panting, he pushed upright, standing over the semi-conscious marshal. He wiped a torn sleeve across his forehead, blotting sweat, staggered slightly as he turned to look after Heck Coburn.

The man was just disappearing over the crest of the sandhill, a faint red haze hanging down the face of the dune to mark his passage. He turned his mount and his voice drifted down faintly to the yard of Brazos Station.

'One — short — hour — Brett!' Then he dropped out of sight.

The deputy went to the well, brought up a pail of water, plunged his bloody, dirty face into it, sloshed the rest over the marshal. The man coughed and spluttered, lay there, gasping as Brett wound up a fresh pail full and poured it over himself. He squeezed water out of his eyes, picked up Needham's six-gun and tossed it towards the man.

'How the hell do you hold onto your marshal's badge, Needham?'

The man picked up his gun, sat up and slowly replaced the used shells with fresh ones from his bullet belt. Without looking up he said quietly, 'Badge-totin' runs in the family. My father was a ranger, my kid brother a deputy in Amarillo ... Pa's been dead for years, Apaches got him — but the kid ... ' He paused and when he continued, he still didn't look up at Brett. 'He drew guard chore on a pay-train from El Paso. Bannerman's bunch jumped it, three months back — three months, eleven days and about ten hours, I reckon ... ' Now he looked up, his swelling eyes haunted. 'Bastard used nitro, just like he did on the La Union train. Never give the guards in the express van any kinda chance to even open up. That kid was the only family I had left in the world, Brett — Bannerman just tossed the nitro bottle through a window he shot out first and it blew like ... ' Again he paused. He had to clear his throat before he could continue. 'There was two walls left standin', roof and the other walls'd been blowed to hell. Them two walls were covered in bits of clothin', stickin' to blood and gore ... I found the kid's gold tooth he was always so proud of, embedded in a plank like it'd been shot there out of a gun. It's the only bit of him I ever found . . . '

Brett said nothing, wiped water from his face with his hands, then stepped forward and offered his right hand to Needham. The marshal ignored it, clambered to his feet himself, face hard.

'Needham — Rose is all *I*'ve got in the world now. I don't aim to lose her . . . '

Needham said nothing, rammed his gun back into its holster. 'We best go through the motions of bringin' up that strongbox, I guess.' He looked steadily at the deputy.

Brett climbed down the bucket rope, taking another rope with him to tie to the handle of the strongbox resting on the underwater ledge. He did so and called to Needham to brace the line so he could climb up: the bucket rope was too wet and slimy. But the dry rope did not go taut as he expected.

'Come on, Needham! Wrap the rope

around the windlass once or twice and hold the loose end so I can climb out.'

'You need coolin' off, Brett.' The marshal's voice came booming down the well to him. And hard on the heels of the lawman's words, the dry rope came snaking down to splash into the water beside Brett. The deputy swore, drew his six-gun.

'Damn you, Needham! Get me out of here! — If you do anything to get Rose harmed I'll . . . ' He couldn't see Needham now.

The marshal didn't answer and Brett's words boomed back at him, hollow, empty . . . He was stranded . . . Helpless . . .

* * *

Lying prone on top of the sandhill, Heck Coburn lowered the field glasses and twisted towards Bannerman where the killer sat beside the silent girl. Rose wasn't bound or restrained in any way.

234

But one side of her face was bruised and a sleeve of her blouse was torn at the shoulder. Her flesh showed bruising from rough handling. She sat with her knees drawn up, head resting on her forearms.

'I dunno what the hell they're doin',' Coburn said. 'Brett went down into the well like before, to tie the rope to the box, I guess — But he ain't come back out. And looked to me like Needham tossed the rope in after him.'

Rose looked up sharply and Bannerman studied the yard carefully. 'Needham's a vindictive sonuver — He didn't like Brett beatin' on him. He's leavin' him down there.'

Coburn frowned. 'Why the hell? He's s'posed to bring that box up for us!'

'Yah — He's up to somethin'. Mebbe they got it rigged so's Brett can come leapin' over the wall and try to get the drop on us . . . ' He tossed the field glasses to Coburn, spun towards the girl and grabbed her by the arm, dragging her across to him. She winced in pain but stifled any cry.

'They try anythin' like that, sweet-heart, an' they're gonna see inside your head!' He stood up just below the crest, face ugly now. 'C'mon, Heck. We're goin' down there!'

* * *

Brett tried to climb the wet windlass rope several times but he only managed to get up a few feet before the slimy strands slid through his tightly gripping hands and he plunged back down to the ledge, waist-deep in water. He couldn't hear anything up above and Needham didn't answer when he called. His gun rig dangled from his shoulder now, clear of the water. He fought rising panic. If Coburn and Bannerman were watching, as they would be, they would wonder what was going on. And Rose could be endangered . . . *Do something*! he told himself.

He grabbed the bucket rope again, hauled up his legs until he could twist them around the strand and tried pulling himself up this way, gaining some extra leverage. He reached almost to the halfway mark before he inevitably slid back once more. Panting, hands raw, arms feeling as if they were pulling out of their sockets, he balanced precariously on top of the heavy strongbox, mind racing, trying to figure a way out of here, toying with the end of the rope tied to the box handle.

The walls were too smooth and slippery to attempt to climb. All the ropes were wet. There wasn't any projection he could lasso with the rope that Needham had dropped down. Damn it, there had to be *some* way . . . And just as he thought of something to try, he heard voices, shouting, arguing, but he couldn't make out the words.

Then suddenly a woman screamed and there followed a crash of gunfire . . .

* * *

Needham stood in the shade of the porch as he watched the two outlaws ride in, the girl straddling the saddle in front of Bannerman. He flicked away his cigarette and moved to the top of the short steps, picking up his rifle and holding it at the ready.

'Give it up, Bannerman!' he called. 'You can't get away with this. I got four men inside coverin' you.'

The outlaws hauled rein without even glancing towards the adobe building where the marshal had jammed one spare rifle and a couple of lengths of old pipe under window frames. Bannerman pressed a cocked pistol against Rose's head and Coburn held his rifle across his thighs, eyes darting about now.

'You're a goddamned liar, Needham,' he said quietly. 'You ain't got no one here but Brett — and you left him down the well — How come?'

The marshal smiled crookedly. 'Because I don't need him just for you two.'

'You're forgettin' Sweetie here,'

Bannerman reminded him, pushing his gun so hard against Rose's head that she was forced to tilt it, making a small moaning sound.

'I ain't forgettin' nothin' — 'specially the way you killed my kid brother!'

Bannerman grinned tightly. 'They tell me there weren't enough left to even feed the coyotes!'

Needham went white, wrenching his rifle up in his rage. Coburn's gun fired, the bullet tearing splinters from the awning post beside the lawman, slivers spearing his face. He reeled, his own shot going wild. Then Bannerman shoved the girl roughly and she screamed in shock as she fell hard to the ground, breath knocked out of her, as the killer hammered three fast shots at Needham. The marshal reeled and staggered down the steps, stumbled, and sprawled on his face in the dust.

Bannerman grinned tightly, pleased, and Coburn turned from looking at the downed lawman to glance towards the well. He stiffened, eyes flying wide, rifle coming up in a blur as he levered a fresh shell into the breech.

'*Watch out!*'

Caleb Brett came hurtling over the well wall as if shot from a cannon, blazing six-gun in his hand as he took in the situation in one wild, raking glance. The main thing was that Rose was well away from Bannerman . . .

He somersaulted, landed on his shoulders, rolling to his knees as bullets spat into the rock wall behind him and tore spurting furrows in the sun-baked ground. He threw himself sideways, triggering as fast as he could cock and fire.

Coburn reared in the stirrups as he rode in, his face destroyed by a bullet taking him under the jaw and angling upwards. Brett twisted towards Bannerman and the outlaw fought his plunging horse, shooting down at the deputy even as Brett's slugs tore into his body, one ripping a large piece out of his throat. He reeled, holding on with the last of his fast-ebbing strength, reared the horse above the sprawled girl in one final attempt to kill her.

But, blood gushing, he rolled back in the saddle, yanking the reins and pulling the horse to the side and back so that it lost balance. It crushed him into the ground as Rose rolled safely out of the way . . .

Brett ran to her, knelt, and held her tightly against his wet shirt, gently stroking her hair, feeling the trembling leave her gradually. Finally, she eased out of his grip, sat back and twisted around to look up into his face.

'What happened? You hurtled out of that well as if shot from a catapult!'

'Just about what happened,' he told her, smiling wearily. 'I tied my six-gun to the rope we'd hitched to the strongbox — which was filled with rocks, by the by: we'd buried the loot under the forge. Anyway, I tossed my six-gun over the winch after a couple of tries and caught it when it carried the rope end down to me. Then I held on tight and kicked the strongbox off the ledge. It plunged straight to the bottom of the well and I shot up and over the stone wall — I was mighty glad to see you out of Bannerman's grip, Rose.'

She kissed him gently on the mouth, snuggling against him and pulling his arms about her. 'Yours is the only grip I ever want to be in, Caleb,' she told him huskily.

He kissed the top of her head. 'Suits me,' he told her, tightening his arms about her soft body.

THE END

Other titles in the Linford Western Library

THE CROOKED SHERIFF
John Dyson

Black Pete Bowen quit Texas with a burning hatred of men who try to take the law into their own hands. But he discovers that things aren't much different in the silver mountains of Arizona.

THEY'LL HANG BILLY FOR SURE:
Larry & Stretch
Marshall Grover

Billy Reese, the West's most notorious desperado, was to stand trial. From all compass points came the curious and the greedy, the riff-raff of the frontier. Suddenly, a crazed killer was on the loose — but the Texas Trouble-Shooters were there, girding their loins for action.

RIDERS OF RIFLE RANGE
Wade Hamilton

Veterinarian Jeff Jones did not like open warfare — but it was there on Scrub Pine grass. When he diagnosed a sick bull on the Endicott ranch as having the contagious blackleg disease, he got involved in the warfare — whether he liked it or not!

BEAR PAW
Nevada Carter

Austin Dailey traded two cows to a pair of Indians for a bay horse, which subsequently disappeared. Tracks led to a secret hideout of fugitive Indians — and cattle thieves. Indians and stockmen co-operated against the rustlers. But it was Pale Woman who acted as interpreter between her people and the rangemen.

THE WEST WITCH
Lance Howard

Detective Quinton Hilcrest journeys west, seeking the Black Hood Bandits' lost fortune. Within hours of arriving in Hags Bend, he is fighting for his life, ensnared with a beautiful outcast the town claims is a witch! Can he save the young woman from the angry mob?

GUNS OF THE PONY EXPRESS
T. M. Dolan

Rich Zennor joined the Pony Express venture at the start, as second-in-command to tough Denning Hartman. But Zennor had the problems of Hartman believing that they had crossed trails in the past, and the fact that he was strongly attached to Hartman's Indian girl, Conchita.

BLACK JO OF THE PECOS
Jeff Blaine

Nobody knew where Black Josephine Callard came from or whither she returned. Deputy U.S. Marshal Frank Haggard would have to exercise all his cunning and ability to stay alive before he could defeat her highly successful gang and solve the mystery.

RIDE FOR YOUR LIFE
Johnny Mack Bride

They rode west, hoping for a new start. Then they met another broken-down casualty of war, and he had a plan that might deliver them from despair. But the only men who would attempt it would be the truly brave — or the desperate. They were both.

THE NIGHTHAWK
Charles Burnham

While John Baxter sat looking at the ruin that arsonists had made of his log house, a stranger rode into the yard. Baxter and Walt Showalter partnered up and re-built the house. But when it was dynamited, they struck back — and all hell broke loose.

MAVERICK PREACHER
M. Duggan

Clay Purnell was hopeful that his posting to Capra would be peaceable enough. However, on his very first day in town he rode into trouble. Although loath to use his .45, Clay found he had little choice — and his likeness to a notorious bank robber didn't help either!

SIXGUN SHOWDOWN
Art Flynn

After years as a lawman elsewhere, Dan Herrick returned to his old Arizona stamping ground to find that nesters were being driven from their homesteads by ruthless ranchers. Before putting away his gun once and for all, Dan forced a bloody and decisive showdown.

RIDE LIKE THE DEVIL!
Sam Gort

Ben Trunch arrived back on the Big T only to find that land-grabbing was in progress. He confronted Luke Fletcher, saloon-keeper and town boss, with what was happening, and was immediately forced to ride for his life. But he got the chance to put it all right in the end.

SLOW WOLF AND DAN FOX:
Larry & Stretch
Marshall Grover

The deck was stacked against an innocent man. Larry Valentine played detective, and his investigation propelled the Texas Trouble-Shooters into a gun-blazing fight to the finish.

BRANAGAN'S LAW
Alan Irwin

To Angus Flint, the valley was his domain and he didn't want any new settlers. But Texas Ranger Jim Branagan had other ideas. Could he put an end to Flint's tyranny for good?

THE DEVIL RODE A PINTO
Bret Rey

When a settler is cut to ribbons in a frenzied attack, Texas Ranger Sam Buck learns that the killer is Rufus Berry, known as The Devil. Sam stiffens his resolve to kill or capture Berry and break up his gang.

THE DEATH MAN
Lee F. Gregson
The hardest of men went in fear of Ford, the bounty hunter, who had earned the name 'The Death Man'. Yet even Ford was not infallible — when he killed the wrong man, he found that he was being sought himself by the feared Frank Ambler.

LEAD LANGUAGE
Gene Tuttle
After Blaze Colton and Ricky Rawlings have delivered a train load of cows from Arizona to San Francisco, they become involved in a load of trouble and find themselves on the run!

A DOLLAR FROM THE STAGE
Bill Morrison
Young saddle-tramp Len Finch stumbled into a web of murder, lawlessness, intrigue and evil ambition. In the end, he put his life on the line for the folks that he cared about.